ROCKY'S

Eulogy

LAWRENCE IANNI

iUniverse, Inc.
Bloomington

Rocky's Eulogy

iUniverse books may be ordered through booksellers or by contacting:

iUniverse
1663 Liberty Drive
Bloomington, IN 47403
www.iuniverse.com
1-800-Authors (1-800-288-4677)

Because of the dynamic nature of the Internet, any Web addresses or links contained in this book may have changed since publication and may no longer be valid. The views expressed in this work are solely those of the author and do not necessarily reflect the views of the publisher, and the publisher hereby disclaims any responsibility for them.

Any people depicted in stock imagery provided by Thinkstock are models, and such images are being used for illustrative purposes only.

Certain stock imagery © Thinkstock.

ISBN: 978-1-4502-7693-1 (sc)
ISBN: 978-1-4502-7692-4 (ebook)

Printed in the United States of America

iUniverse rev. date: 1/19/2011

For Laura, who goes her own way and doesn't quit

With admiration for Emily Dickinson, who wrote, "This is my letter to the World/That never wrote to Me---"

Chapter 1

The freedom of retirement had been a disappointment to Anthony Rocco, who was known to the friends of his youth as Rocky. He had earned his nickname as an athlete with few skillful attributes who compensated with an abundance of aggressiveness. That aggressiveness had been useful during his working life after he managed to regulate it for application when faced with hostility, incompetence or devious intent. In retirement, aggression was not only useless but a considerable liability. Rocky's retirement was devoted to recreation and leisure, as he had hoped, but neither activity was as satisfying as he had expected.

He and his wife had always been avid museum goers, but now he found no joy in art that was beautiful and only irritation in art that was intended to shock.

He had anticipated that the time to play as much golf as he wanted would bring happiness. It did not. Greater frequency at golfing turned the game into a fatiguing chore. He reluctantly drew the conclusion that, if he ever had any capacity for joy, he had lost it.

In the three years since he had given up a busy career in university teaching and administration, he found that free time could be a burden rather than a chance to relax.

Rocky had given no forethought to the one circumstance that did not change when his working life ended. He still had to get along with people. While a wage earner, he was forced to admit in moments of candor that he was probably the last person of his generation to develop a modicum of skill in cooperation and compromise. Why he had thought that retirement meant that those skills could be retired too now seemed incredibly naïve. Since retiring, Rocky cooperated and compromised with churlish reluctance. Hence, he now rarely lived a day without experiencing times of irritation followed by regret. He was now alternatively a slave to two emotions: anger and depression.

Rocky was democratic in feeling displeasure. He daily felt it with service people that he had need of and government functionaries whom he could not avoid. He was even unable to suppress his grumpiness in his daily interactions with his wife of forty-three years, who had given up her own career in teaching at the same time Rocky had retired. Being annoyed with his wife magnified the feeling that everything in his life was wrong. He began to doubt that he and Beatrice had ever been compatible. Perhaps they had just been so busy that their interactions had been limited to a necessary minimum that prevented conflict. Now that they spent a great deal more time together sharing chores and activities, their fundamental incompatibility seemed obvious.

The constant conflict got him down. He was unhappy about being unhappy. He did not want to be at sword's point with strangers all the time. This was even more the case with those he loved. He finally concluded that others were not the problem; he was. And he could not change. In fact, he had no desire to change. The thought of continuing in this life bore down on him heavily. The dreariness of his future deepened his already dark moods.

Rocky concluded that his situation was not one that could be remedied by dialogue but only by action. Therefore he had developed a plan that he would soon act upon. Soon, at age sixty-eight, he was going disappear from his life of daily, niggling discontent. He could no longer tolerate his life consisting of an endless succession of minor annoyances. His calmer moments brought the realization that most of his discontent was self-induced, but that did not make it more tolerable. It was past time to cut loose of it.

By simply escaping into a new identity, he would establish a solitary and peaceful life somewhere else than the paid-for California bungalow into which a substantial retirement income flowed every month. He knew that there was one portion of their nest egg he could secretly convert to cash to begin his new life. He could cash in a small, paid up insurance policy without its either being noticed by his wife or injuring her security after he left. He expected to find some kind of unskilled job for which his slightly diminished physical capacities would be adequate. He did not begrudge his wife the entirety of income they had built together. Heaven knew she deserved every penny. He expected that the pay from his new labor alone would permit him to live frugally after the funds he started out with were gone. No doubt he would miss the creature comforts funded by a lifetime of frugality and the joint earnings of him and his wife. But he hoped that a life free from the dissatisfactions that plagued him would more than make up for the loss of the easy living.

Unbeknown to his wife of forty-three years, he had already cashed in the smallest of several paid up life insurance policies. He had concealed the slender packets of one hundred dollar bills in preparation for his departure. He was unsure that the twenty thousand dollars would be an adequate amount to carry out his re-location. But that doubt would not deter him from acting on his plan.

Rocky planned to seize on an unexpected opportunity to disappear without being immediately missed. He was scheduled several weeks hence to fly across country for a reunion with his college football teammates. Since this event was the latest in a succession of such reunions over a thirty year period, his wife Beatrice, who was never really fond of attending them with him, had pleaded not to accompany him. When she insisted that she be excused after patiently having endured the past noisy affairs with forced good humor, Rocky had to struggle not to show his pleasure in accepting her reasoning. She had removed the last obstacle to his putting his desire to disappear into action.

After he had scheduled his flight from San Francisco to Pittsburgh, he expected that skipping the reunion would give him three days to disappear before his wife missed him. He planned to pay cash for a used pick up truck and drive south from Pittsburgh. He had a general idea of the circumstances he was looking for in a place to live and work. When he found a town and job that felt right, he would try to establish himself. If that spot didn't work out in a few months, he would move on again. He meant to continue the process until he was satisfied that he could live in modest comfort and peace.

For almost a year now, Rocky had been convinced he should disappear. Most people would consider the life he was leading since retiring pleasant enough, Rocky supposed. His income was ample to cover basic needs and occasional luxuries for him and his wife. He could not say that he lacked any material thing that he desperately wanted. But, he was tired of perpetual discontent. He concluded, "I make everyone unhappy and myself unhappiest of all. I have only two moods—angry and depressed. Best for all and for me that I go."

Rocky did not delude himself that he had extraordinary strength or vitality for one his age, but he was neither perpetually exhausted or decrepit. He was convinced he could manage to support himself in a hand-to-mouth way. For months he sought for a way to leave and not have his absence noticed immediately. The reunion was the first opportunity that occurred.

As the time for his reunion trip neared, Rocky took his roll-aboard travel case down from the shelf in the garage. Opening the nylon flap that covered the shallow space between the two support pipes into which the handle collapsed, he lay his horde of cash inside the inch deep space and fixed the nylon covering back into place. He had just done the most important part of the packing for his one-way trip three weeks hence.

Chapter 2

Two weeks before his pretended reunion trip, Rocky received a letter written on behalf of the reunion organizing committee. It contained a request that he realized would complicate his escape plan unless he declined the task. The letter informed Rocky that Dave Christianson, the teammate and friend most fondly admired by Rocky and all of Dave's other football teammates, who had died about a year and a half ago, would be eulogized at the reunion. Rocky was being asked to deliver the eulogy of Dave at the reunion.

Some special notice of Dave's passing was unquestionably merited. Not only had Christianson been the most popular member of the team during their playing days, but he was also the man who had single-handedly organized the first several reunions. Later, Dave had energetically led the group of former players who had come to his assistance when the growth of the periodic reunion endeavor made the burden of organizing the event too much of a task for Dave and his wife. Rocky, as had all Dave's other friends, had felt genuine sadness at Christianson's death. Dave held a unique place in the affections of Rocky and all of Dave's football teammates and college acquaintances. He had been a good athlete, although not stellar. He had been a highly respected team leader. More importantly, Christianson had already, as a young collegian, been mature and upright in his behavior when his friends were still searching to discover their long-term values and how they ought to behave as adults. It was Christianson who rescued them several times from the threat of discipline from college officials and local law enforcement when a rescue or mitigation seemed an impossibility.

Christianson never judged them and was generally amused by their harmless foolishness. While the rest of them, in the grip of their hormones rather than their good sense, were childishly aggressive or embarrassingly crude toward women, Dave was courteous and amiable toward female students. His demeanor made him the most popular man on campus with coeds. Yet as engaging as he was, both for his friendliness and his considerable physical attractiveness, his friendships with women were nothing more than that. He made it well known that he remained loyal to his high school sweetheart Carla, later to be his wife, who attended another college several hours distance from their own campus.

Although the program of the group's reunions usually consisted of reminiscences colored with playful distortions laboring toward humor, noting the passing of friends who had been part of the group was customarily the case. Adam Standish, writing on behalf of the committee, wrote that he was sure that everyone would agree that Dave's passing ought to be given more extensive and thoughtful treatment in the program than the usual brief mention. Therefore, the committee was requesting of Rocky that he deliver a eulogy of Dave at the reunion. Under normal circumstances, the task was one that Rocky would have welcomed because of his personal affection for Dave Christianson. However, since he intended to skip the event despite having made a reservation, he intended to respond with some excuse for declining the task.

As he sat down to write his reply declining to deliver the eulogy, Rocky realized that the new circumstances offered the opportunity to improve his disappearance plan if he were willing to add another piece of misinformation to his deception of his wife. Beatrice also knew Dave from her college days and, like everyone else, was fond of him. If he told Beatrice that he was going to deliver the eulogy that he actually meant to beg off from, he could offer a plausible reason to his wife for adding a week to the trip. This early departure would give additional time to disappear before his disappearance would be noted.

Rocky realized that, if he told Beatrice that he had to leave a week earlier to gather sentiments from among Dave's friends to include in the eulogy, he could more than double his time to disappear before he might be sought. Beatrice would not contest that Dave's eulogy deserved a special effort. An appropriate memorial statement about Dave should express the feelings of individual members of the group about him. Beatrice would agree that Rocky should meet before the event with some of their college classmates and Dave's teammates and collect reminiscences that he could incorporate into his eulogy.

This would be a plausible excuse to begin his trip earlier than originally planned. Rocky would assert that he would need time to travel around the Pittsburgh area and meet with some of Dave's college friends, particularly those who had remained close to him over the years since graduation. If he made this case to Beatrice even though he was actually going to reject the assignment, he could depart a week earlier and have ten or eleven days to disappear before he was missed.

Rocky felt small for wanting to take advantage of the situation. He would have liked to be the one to honor Dave Christianson. Rocky would have preferred that the merits of the man be stated as he saw them. He deferred to none of his college acquaintance in respect for what Christianson had done with his life, not only as a collegian but during a long career as an educator. He was honestly concerned that someone else's effort would understate the true worth of the man. However, he felt that his need to facilitate his escape from his situation justified his taking advantage. When Beatrice came home from visiting one of her infirm friends, he would initiate his ploy.

To Rocky's astonishment, Beatrice reacted very favorably to his proposing an earlier departure on his trip. Then his spirits sank when she explained why. "I want to go along if you're going to do some visiting with friends of our college days," she grinned broadly. "And besides, I have relatives in the area I could visit with when you're meeting with people I didn't know all that well." This surprising development left Rocky struggling to respond.

He stared at his wife of forty-three years. "Even if it means going to the reunion dinner that you've always found so boring?"

Beatrice smiled playfully. "To see friends from college days that I haven't seen for years, I'll make the sacrifice." Rocky realized it would be difficult to talk her out of going. Her happiness at the prospect of seeing old friends was apparent. Not only were some of the former athletes acquaintances of hers, but some had married women who had been friends of hers. It made sense that after skipping the last several reunions Beatrice would want to see them. Rocky had failed to anticipate that separate chances to socialize beyond the dinner itself would make the trip more appealing to Beatrice.

Rocky studied his wife's smiling face. It was rarely that he now looked at her closely. He had to admit that Beatrice had the prettiest face of any woman of her age that he knew. With time, her body had, as had his own, taken on weight, perhaps aiding her face to remain smooth. Her healthy complexion glowed with a faint blush. When she showed the animation that a subject of interest aroused, as she did now, her face came near to that of the young woman who had captivated him. How ardently he had pursued her. How reluctantly she had been caught. Through the years, she had been kind rather than loving. It had seemed more than enough. He felt that it still would be enough if her kindness were not now reserved for others than him. He did not know why he was the exception. He no longer cared to struggle with the question.

Beatrice began to put away the groceries she had stopped for after her visit with her homebound friend. Rocky trailed behind her. "I thought that you hated these reunions, especially since a lot of the women that you knew in college are widows now and don't come any more," he said, struggling to keep any pleading quality out of his voice.

"Oh, I can tolerate going to the reunion if the trip also includes not only visiting friends but also a chance to see the relatives that I have in that area. It's four years since I've seen my brother Josh, my Uncle Carl, my aunts and my cousins that live around there. Maybe I could even get them together for a family picnic."

Since he found his in-laws largely amiable, Rocky could think of only the most farfetched resistance to Beatrice's plan. "Kind of short notice to get a family gathering organized, isn't it?"

"Not really, I can make a few phone calls. Lots of them are retired too and likely to be available. They'll welcome something to do for an afternoon. Besides, if I can't organize a group event, we can at least visit some of them. We'd be traveling around there anyway, wouldn't we?

Rocky's spirits sank further. He was about to be trapped into performing a task that he had only meant to pretend to do. To complicate matters further, his selection of people to talk to about Christianson's eulogy was going to determined by his informants' proximity to Beatrice's relatives. Not only was his plan to disappear about to be foiled but also the entire trip was about to follow the pattern that produced the gnawing discontent of the life he was desperate to leave behind. Since retiring, he never got to do exactly what he wanted to do. What he did was never more than an approximation of what he wanted to do because his original plan was compromised to mesh with some desire that Beatrice grafted on to his original intent.

He capped his smoldering anger. "Well, why don't you think about it overnight before you decide. There's not much time to see if your folks are available, and it would be a shame to make a trip and end up not seeing your relatives after all." His reasoning sounded lame as he said it. What were the odds the several of Beatrice's elderly and practically home bound relatives would not be accessible to be visited. Even her brother Josh was retired and no doubt could be visited almost any time.

The next morning, he did not have to ask if Beatrice had reconsidered. When he returned from his daily walk, Beatrice told him that she had changed his plane reservation and gotten them a flight together. "I'd better get busy," Beatrice said, her voice rising in excitement. "I'll make some phone calls and see about a time and place for a family picnic. Of course, we'll be renting a car, won't we? If we can't have a family gathering, I'll tell people that we'll be stopping by to see them during that week."

Actually, he hadn't made a car reservation. He had planned to take a cab from the airport to the nearest used car lot and be on his way south toward freedom in a few hours. Now he would actually be visiting people to collect reminiscences and sentiments for Dave's eulogy. He too now needed to make a phone call. He would call Adam

Standish, the man who had written to request that he do the eulogy, to say that he was accepting the task.

In addition, he should discuss with Adam if he knew who among Christianson's friends lived at or near the locations where Beatrice's relatives lived. Although Rocky and Dave had shared many friends in college, he expected that his choice of Dave's friends to visit would be determined by their living near Beatrice's relatives rather than the reverse. The family visits undoubtedly would become the primary consideration for their travels. He would have to plan around Beatrice's desires rather than having his task determine whether relatives would be visited.

Rocky sighed and began to organize his task in his mind. Life as usual, he reflected silently. Never a catastrophe, never an unalloyed joy. Always the slightly stale cake, and the wrong recipe as well.

Chapter 3

As Rocky maneuvered the rented car through the confusingly labeled access roads out of the Pittsburgh airport, he wondered if the signs were better guides to local users of the airport that they were for strangers. Of course, his uneasiness was compounded by Beatrice's continuous suggestions, to which she expected instantaneous responses even if he had just committed to another option. This was a condition that Rocky was familiar with as a feature of driving with his wife as a passenger. Nevertheless, his body temperature and anxiety rose along with his uncertainty. He rarely complained about Beatrice's incessant orders while he drove. Occasionally, she kept him from making a dangerous error or a time-consuming mistake. Yet the stream of directions was an irritation because the comments were most often unnecessary.

Sometimes the instructions undermined his confidence in a correct choice he had just made and cause a momentary paralysis. Beatrice occasionally asserted that they would die of one of his driving mistakes. Rocky thought that the odds were just as great that the confusion she created would one day result in a serious accident. Rocky's policy was to try to maintain silence in the face of the steady stream of directions. Rationality reminded him that her saving him from an occasional mistake was an acceptable trade off for the irritation of constantly being directed to do what he was usually in the process of doing anyway. He took some perverse pride in not saying a word to Beatrice about her driving when he was her passenger. Actually she was a good and careful driver. Yet she did made her share of mistakes. Wisdom suggested to Rocky that silence would at least prevent a dialogue in which a response enumerating his real and imagined sins would overshadow the legitimacy of his having called an error to notice.

Rocky did not delude himself that his silence represented a stance of moral superiority. He was simply avoiding a deeper quagmire. He had adopted this practice of refraining to criticize from his study of a twelve step program. Retaliation against criticism is corrosive, it counseled. He hoped that restraint did make substance abusers feel better. He, however, did not find that it elevated his spirits. Simmering in silence merely strengthened the feeling that his life was like perpetually having a nail in his shoe.

Why did he try to avoid the game of tit for tat? Because he always lost it when he was tempted to play. Rocky recognized that he had reached the stage in life where there occurred what he called the universal old people's dialogue. In this scenario, one person said something like, "My back is sore." Among the elderly, the complaint was always responded to with something like, "I had a sore back last week that was really excruciating." Sympathy becomes a rarity when pain is common to all. Since Rocky was as prone to engage in the pattern of dialogue as any other oldster, the only way to avoid the irritating result altogether was not to initiate it or respond to a complaint with one of one's own.

Once he was certain of his route toward their destination, Rocky began to relax as much as it was possible with Beatrice as his passenger. He expected that at least the beginning of the trip would be pleasant. It was only an hour and a half drive to what was likely to be a comfortable motel at which they had reservations for the night. The next day they would visit Rocky's favorite among Beatrice's relatives. Beatrice's Uncle Carl, more than twenty years Rocky's senior, resided in an assisted living facility. Since he was wheelchair bound, his pastimes were limited to smoking his pipe while he watched sports on television. Some additional zest was added his televiewing if there was a bit of brandy in the coffee that he sipped as he watched. Since Uncle Carl's means were modest, Rocky did not find it very expensive to upgrade the quality of the brandy that Uncle Carl tipped into the strong black coffee that he favored.

Rocky had come prepared to add to the old man's supply of coffee enrichment. After the first sampling, Uncle Carl would be prepared to launch into his assessment of the perpetual helplessness of the Pittsburgh Pirates, whom he had followed devotedly for practically all of his eighty-eight years. Because Rocky had retained his own devotion to the Pirates despite his having lived on the west coast for years, he had his own perceptions to share about his and Uncle Carl's mutually frustrating interest.

Rocky also intended tomorrow to have his first meeting to get material for his eulogy of Dave Christianson. In Belleville, a town a few miles from the facility where Beatrice's Uncle Carl lived, there lived a woman named R. Madeline Summerfield who had been suggested by the reunion planners as a likely source of input. Rocky did not recognize the woman's name from his college days. Either she was a college contemporary about whose marriage he had not heard or she was someone with whom Dave had been associated in his career after college. If they spent the morning with Uncle Carl and took him out to lunch, he would probably be exhausted and need a nap by the time they brought him back from the restaurant. Rocky gauged he would be free to meet with Ms. Summerfield in mid afternoon.

When he phoned that evening from the motel to ask for an appointment the next afternoon, he began quite formally to explain who he was. His explanation was interrupted by a gravelly and loud interjection. "You dumb dago, Tony Rocco, why would you think I'd need to be reminded who your sorry ass is?

Both the voice and the rhetoric were familiar but he could not quite place them. More meekly than he would usually respond to being called by an epithet that always raised his blood, Rocky queried meekly, "I'm sorry?"

"You should be, you stupid wop. This is Ronnie--Rhonda Barrett."

"Rhonda," Rocky repeated slowly, not for want of immediate recognition, but from surprise. "Rhonda, of course I remember you. Who wouldn't remember? You were unforgettable. I wasn't given any maiden name information, so I didn't know it was you. The listing I have just says R. Madeline Summerfield."

Rocky did not exaggerate in calling Rhonda unforgettable. She had been a prominent and flamboyant figure on campus during their college days. Blessed with an extraordinary singing voice and a prima donna's temperament, Rhonda clamored to be the center of attention wherever she appeared, whether it was in the coffee bar of the student union or among the students milling about between classes. She was quite justly featured in musical recitals and theatricals. She carried her dominating stage presence into the daily routine of campus life. She was an outrageous flirt. However, she never privately went beyond teasing though she was lavish with her public hugs and kisses, which she reserved for males whom she judged would not be prompted to make serious advances. Personally, Rocky had never thought the product would live up to its advertising. He hadn't to worry that he would ever be invited to sample it. Rhonda had assessed Rocky as a dangerous and unrefined commodity. However, she was as civil to him as her flamboyant rhetoric would permit because she liked many of the males among his friends, especially with whom her flirtatiousness was never in danger of actually proceeding to anything more. There were innumerable things that Rocky would rather do than spend an hour with Ronnie Barrett. However, she was a good candidate to provide an interesting perception of Dave Christianson, whom Rhonda had responded to in lively fashion years ago.

Rocky was no longer sensitive to the ethnic slur with which Rhonda had assailed him with over the phone. Besides, she was merely reverting to the sarcastic style that had been the usual mode of dialogue between her and Rocky decades ago. Rocky responded that he was glad to hear how delightfully she had mellowed with age. Thus four decades disappeared in a minute.

He then explained why he wanted to meet with her. Rhonda said that she had only heard several days ago of the death of "Davey," as she called him, her term being a diminutive of the shortening of "David" that Christianson's male friends used. Rhonda said that she was anxious to contribute to the eulogy; however, she was not available tomorrow afternoon, the time he had requested. Why didn't he come mid-morning tomorrow, she asked. Rocky consulted with Beatrice to ask if he could leave her to visit with her uncle alone in the morning if he joined them in time to take them to lunch. Beatrice was agreeable, so Rocky told Rhonda that he would see her at ten in the morning as she had suggested.

In the morning, with Rhonda's directions, Rocky found her home easily. However, when the door opened in response to his ringing the bell, he was surprised to find not Rhonda but another of his college contemporaries, Freddie Picolino.

"Hello, Rocky," Freddie smiled. Freddie stepped aside from the door, bent from the waist in a theatrical bow and invited Rocky in with a sweeping gesture of one arm.

"Nice to see you, Freddie. I didn't realize you'd be here. It's fortunate you are. Rhonda's probably told you what I'm doing, so I'm glad to have a chance to get your input too."

Rocky stepped into a sizeable foyer and looked around. Along the opposite wall was a table on which stood a large bouquet of blue and white delphiniums. Above them was an oil portrait of a portly middle elderly man with a round face and smooth features. Aware that Rocky was studying the picture, Freddie explained, "Ronnie's husband Henry Summerfield. Dead for six years now."

Rocky's turning to look at Freddie must have suggested to him that Rocky was about to ask a question. "No, no," Freddie said with a dismissive wave. "Ronnie and I are just friends. We've enjoyed spending time together since we both lost our spouses." Actually, if Rocky had said anything, it would have been that the man in the picture seemed a surprising choice of spouse for the Ronnie Barrett he remembered. His silence was fortunate, since he might have unguardedly added that Freddie seemed an equally improbable successor.

"I'm glad you both have avoided loneliness," Rocky said. "Is Ronnie still as flamboyant and stagy as she used to be?" Rocky's question was worded in accord with general campus perception rather than in the less kind terminology that would have been his own choice.

"She still has her moments," Freddie laughed. "But, you know, Rocky, we've all changed from those days." Rocky sensed the beginning of a story that he did not want to hear. "She's only occasionally the old Ronnie."

"I see," Rocky nodded and forestalled more on a subject that was more personal than he cared to hear about. He looked around wondering at Rhonda's not having appeared.

"Ronnie's not home at the moment, Rocky," Freddie explained. "She went to pick up something at a tailor shop. She'll be back shortly."

"Maybe that's just as well, Freddie. You and I can chat about Dave for a few minutes then."

Freddie waved Rocky into a spacious living room and motioned him toward the couch and sat in a chair facing him. "I can't be much help to you, Rocky. I knew Dave and thought he was a great guy, just like everyone else. But I never got close to him as you jocks did."

"The college was so small in those days, Freddie," Rocky prompted. "You had to be around for some of the foolishness. You remember how Ronnie used to put guys on. Were you ever around when Ronnie was using her vamp routine to have fun with Dave?"

"Fun wasn't exactly what you guys used to call it then."

Rocky smiled as he recalled a term he had not heard, let alone used in decades. "Ah, yes," he grinned, "ball breaking." It was a term used to describe the actions of a girl who indulged in elaborate but unfelt public displays of affection that would inevitably lead to disappointment if a male took them seriously. A coed who behaved thus was called a ball breaker. The ball referred to was not an implement used in any sport but a crucial and sensitive part of the male anatomy. The term was perhaps a bit unfair, for it was applied to both serious sexual teasers as well as women who merely roll-played at stirring male passion. Ronnie was one of the latter. Yet inexperienced young males might have been forgiven for not distinguishing between Ronnie's dramatic and insincere brassiness and actual sexual teasing that resulted in distracting frustration.

Freddie gazed at Rocky seriously. "I'd recommend staying away from the term now, Rocky."

Rocky smiled reassuringly. "It's been a long time, Freddie. I'm sure none of us behave now in accord with the self-image we projected back then."

"Most of all you, I understand," said Freddie.

"I'm no masterpiece of maturation, Freddie. It just wasn't possible to stay as angry as I was back then, especially since I could never remember exactly what I'd been so perpetually mad about in college."

"You used to drive Phil nuts," referring to one of Rocky's teammates who was a friend of Freddie.

"Phil liked Dave, though," Rocky said, eager to change the subject.

"Dave kept you and Phil from fighting in practice one day, didn't he?" Freddie smiled.

"He did," said Rocky. "Funny. I started after Phil. I can't remember why. I only needed half a reason in those days," Rocky said with a shake of his head. "One of the coaches yelled for me to stop. I never slowed down. But when Dave called my name, I stopped dead." Rocky exhaled deeply. "He was that kind of guy. You just listened to him. Thanks for reminding me of that, Freddie. That's the kind of thing I want to say about Dave. I owe you one."

"How about if I collect right away?"

"Name it," said Rocky, raising his hands palm up in an accepting gesture.

"When Ronnie comes back, she's going to have the shirts she had made for our college singing group--you remember the Cougarland Quartet--to wear when we sing at the re-union."

"Of course I remember the quartet," Rocky said. "You've sung at every reunion I've been to. God, Freddie, you don't want me to sing with you guys, I hope; I can't carry a tune."

"No, no. No offense, Rocky, but you're the last person Ronnie would want to have sing with us." Freddie looked at Rocky apprehensively, perhaps recalling the quick temper for which Rocky was noted in college. "It's the shirts, Rocky. You remember the school colors, blue and gold. Ronnie's had blue shirts made for us to wear with white slacks."

"Sounds fine to me."

"How about gold sequins on the shirts? We'll look like an Atlantic City lounge act." Freddie said resignedly.

Rocky laughed heartily. Freddie looked wounded. The sharp nosed, weak-chinned face recalled for Rocky the fussiness that had been Freddie's distinguishing trait years ago.

"It's not funny, Rocky," Freddie said gravely. "I'm an elementary school principal. I do have an image to maintain. I'm a public figure. My picture is in the paper all the time."

"A few sequins can't be the end of the world, Freddie."

"Maybe not, but you could do me a favor if you just told Ronnie when she comes in with them that they're not a good idea."

"Freddie, Ronnie's attitude about me probably hasn't changed since college. My criticizing those shirts would be all that's needed to increase Ronnie's determination to use them."

"Just give it a try, Rocky, please," Freddie beseeched.

"Why don't you object yourself, Freddie?"

"Actually, Ronnie's already annoyed with me about the shirts. I was supposed to pick up the shirts at the tailor, but I lost the ticket. Ronnie thinks I did it on purpose."

"And you didn't," Rocky suggested, "did you?"

"Not consciously," Freddie nodded. "But things get complicated between me and Ronnie sometimes."

"Do you and Ronnie have a serious relationship, Freddie?"

"We're both widowed, you know. We do see one another regularly. Or perhaps I should say regularly between arguments."

"You two? Navigating the rocky course of love, Freddie?" Rocky said with unconcealed amusement.

"Neither of us would want to call our relationship 'love', Rocky. Let's say we're friends; friends who'll have a lot better chance of remaining that way for the reunion if you can convince her to forget the sequined shirts." Freddie looked at Rocky pleadingly.

Rocky understood the foolhardiness of giving the advice that he was tempted to give. Besides, considering his own faltering marital relationship, he did not feel well qualified to offer any kind of relationship advice. However, he could see no personal risk in helping Freddie "Why not?" Rocky acceded. "I'll give it a shot." 'Shot' was the operative word, thought Rocky regarding the verbal consequence of his efforts.

Moments later, C. Madeline 'Ronnie' Summerfield returned home. Dangling from her upraised hand encased in a clear plastic cover were four electric blue shirts. The outermost one sparkled with a sash-like band of gold sequins descending from one shoulder and extending diagonally across the front of the shirt down to the waist.

Rocky rose to greet his tardy hostess and smiled warily as a stocky female form with a familiar squarish face approached him. Her hair was curled rather than being lengthy and straight as he remembered. There was no mistaking the voice, however, as she railed, "Well, you decrepit excuse for a man, you're here."

"You're as keenly observant as ever, Ronnie," Rocky said. "And still overflowing with expressions of kindness toward your fellow man."

"Don't be a smart ass; you can't pull off the smart part," Ronnie challenged and dropped the shirts over the back of a chair. She sat down and looked doubtful. "So you going to do Davey's eulogy?"

"Maybe not. When I tell the committee about those god awful shirts you're planning to wear to sing, they'll probably cancel the re-union."

"I'm not interested in what you think of the shirts."

Undeterred, Rocky charged ahead. "First of all, that blinding blue is miles off from the college's color. Of course, I do commend you for the sequins. a little subtle as a statement of gay pride, but I think our group will get it."

"You always were a tasteless bastard, Rocky."

"Where I come from, a reference to gay pride could never be in bad taste. However, I think any statement from you about taste is more a peculiarity than a reasoned judgment. But let me not dwell further on these pleasantries. What would you like me to say about Dave, who, you may recall, did not care for the diminutive form of his name."

"Everyone called him 'Davey'," asserted Ronnie.

"Actually only his women acquaintances did."

"Maybe we gave him the softer name because he was the only one of your group who wasn't a grabby pig."

"I wasn't aware of any of them grabbing at you, but let's not continue down this route to old animosities. Freddie was there. Surely he met your standard of decorum."

"Freddie knows I didn't mean him. He has always been very nice." Ronnie reached over and patted Freddie on the cheek.

"He's more than nice," said Rocky. "Otherwise why would he be willing to wear that tacky shirt to sing at the re-union?"

"He likes that shirt, don't you, Freddie."

Freddie's eyes darted back and forth between Ronnie and Rocky. His face showed the struggle between agreeability and his true feelings. "Maybe it wouldn't hurt to ask Max and Harriet what they think," Freddie offered, referring to the other two members of the quartet.

Ronnie's irritated expression showed Rocky that she was now no more patient with resistance to her will than she had been forty plus years ago. She stared at Freddie intensely. Freddie did not wither, Rocky noted. Nor was he gearing for battle. Ronnie gave no sign of attacking. Rocky concluded that this was their usual mode of dealing with disagreement until time brought a thaw in the chilly silence. Rocky managed not to reveal his amusement as the pair settled into their entrenched mental positions. Each looked resolved to wait out a long period of wordless hostility.

Rocky decided that now was a good time to tell them that he was due to join Beatrice and her aged uncle for lunch. With awkward cheerfulness, he said that he would see them at the re-union. As an afterthought he suggested that if they had any thoughts about what they would like to have said about Dave they could jot it down and give it to him before his speech at the re-union. Rocky accepted their terse farewells as he hastened to exit.

The day took on a decidedly more pleasant mood when Rocky walked into the reception area of the assisted living facility where Beatrice and her Uncle Carl waited to be taken to lunch. Carl looked up from the sports magazine that he had been reading and said, "Big news, Tony," the old man said with mischief in his eye "Ray Arrias has raised his average all the way to .245. At his salary, that's about $10,000 per hit."

"What's the difference; there's no one on base when he gets a hit anyway, Uncle Carl," Rocky responded, spreading his arms resignedly. "The team's last in the league in runs scored."

Carl wheeled his chair toward Rocky and stuck out his hand. "We had this conversation three years ago the last time you were here." Uncle Carl chuckled,

Rocky matched the elderly man's firm grip and said, "That team never changes. Even when they change players it never changes."

"I hope it never does," said Uncle Carl. "The shock might kill me."

"You're tough enough to withstand such a shock. Besides," added Rocky, "I've got some of that California elixir of life for you in my suitcase."

"More of that good brandy?" the old man asked with a broad smile. "It takes me a year to get used to my usual stuff after I've worked on a bottle of what you bring me."

"I wish he wouldn't bring you any, Uncle Carl," Beatrice said. "You shouldn't be drinking at all."

"Don't you remember what your father used to say, Beatrice?" asked Carl. He put on a judicial face and intoned, "A man's a fool if he drinks before fifty and a fool if he doesn't drink after fifty."

Rocky nodded, "Yeh, but Jack never really could get the hang of it even when he was past fifty."

"That's the truth," said Carl as he turned to his niece. "Your dad almost never took a drink. The only flaw in an otherwise exemplary character."

"You haven't yet lived as long as he did, you know," Beatrice chided affectionately. She proceeded to hand Carl the straw hat she'd been holding. "Come on, let's get some lunch into you. That will do you a lot more good than what Rocky has in his suitcase." She checked to see that the brake on the wheel chair was released and that Carl's feet were on the foot rests. With a nod to Rocky to manage the chair, she held the door open so that they could proceed to the car.

On their arrival at the restaurant. Beatrice solicitously gave Rocky directions on where to park to facilitate Carl's movements most easily. With his comfort in mind, she chose the table, encouraged his choice of his favorite food and anticipated his every need throughout the meal. Rocky smiled at the unaffected care and kindness that Beatrice showed her uncle. It was in this kindness that he found Beatrice at her best. In that, he noted, she had not changed in the more than four decades since he had first met her. Beatrice continued her kindnesses to her invalid uncle until the moment they left him. Rocky concluded that his wife had lost none of her sensitivity over the years; he simply was no longer the recipient of it.

Chapter 4

The next morning, Beatrice dropped Rocky off to spend most of the day with one of the closest friends he shared with Dave Christianson. She drove on to visit with one of her cousins whom Rocky had only met twice during his entire life. The woman took no offense at Rocky's visiting an old friend rather than spending the day listening to her and Beatrice discuss family members about whom Rocky had scant acquaintance and less interest. That he and his wife had separate plans was fortunate for Rocky. The man was not a particular favorite of Beatrice, who much preferred visiting family. However, Frank Atkinson was someone Rocky would have wanted to see even if he did not have the task of collecting Atkinson's thoughts on their mutual friend Dave Christianson.

Frank was sitting on his porch drinking a mid-morning cup of coffee when Rocky came up the walk to Atkinson's home. He greeted Frank and explained why Beatrice, who needed to hurry on if she was to have a full day with her cousin, had waved briefly and driven off. Marcie Atkinson emerged from the house to offer Rocky a cup of coffee. Rocky declined the offer and passed on Beatrice's greeting. Marcie asked if "Treece" as Beatrice was known to all during her college days would be at the at the re-union the coming Saturday. Rocky assured her of that and Marcie disappeared to let the two old friends to visit.

Rocky always enjoyed his infrequent conversations with Frank, though he found one aspect of their talks puzzling. Rocky always expected Atkinson, who had had a long and successful career in the steel industry, to speak of his former work on occasion. Most men spoke of their life's work in the course of conversation. Indeed, some did so more extensively than a listener cared to hear, but Frank Atkinson never did other than to make a terse response to any direct question.

Perhaps the most impressive part of that career had been Frank's having managed the computerization of the steel manufacturing process at his particular plant of the huge nationwide corporation. Frank had overseen the computerization of every stage of the plant's operation. That included everything from the acquisition of raw materials, through the steel making process to the inventory and shipping phases of the operation. Rocky knew of this only from brief responses that Frank had made to persistent questioning that Rocky injected as diversions from what was invariably the exclusive topic of conversation between the two former college friends.

The almost exclusive subject of their conversation was professional football. Like Frank, Rocky was a fan, but his interest had dwindled through the years so that only the efforts of his lifelong favorite team, the Pittsburgh Steelers, held any interest. Even that interest was short-lived and periodic if the team was having a less than competitive season; Frank, on the other hand, had a more intense interest in all of professional football than ever. His interest was broad. He avidly read a number of magazines on professional football. His primary interest shifted periodically from team to team depending on one factor. Frank admired winning football coaches.

He believed that there were enormous differences in the wisdom and knowledge of various coaches. Like the vast majority of fans, he saw the success or failure of a team determined by the judgment and tactical astuteness of the coach. By mid-season, Frank would decide who was the best coach in the pros and would adopt that team. Of course, since a coach's wisdom was defined by winning, no rational person could tell whether it was the coach's tactics or the skill and aggressiveness of the players that had brought a team a championship. But even here Frank and the believers in coaching genius were not at a loss to determine the cause of success. The coach had chosen the players; hence the coach was a genius at appraising talent.

Members of this cult of admiration discounted the relevance of such factors as injuries to key players or a lack of self-discipline in some well-paid man-child which damaged his performance, or the unpredictable bounces of the ball which sometimes did as much to determine the outcome of games as did the choice of some clever tactic by the coach, or, finally, the failure of the players to execute what had been a perfectly appropriate choice of tactics. All these factors were discounted by the believers in the cult of the current preeminent coaching genius, despite the hard reality that all the coaching geniuses of a half decade or decade ago had grew stupid when a particular group of gifted and determined players aged.

Still, despite disagreeing with Frank Atkinson on what produced winning football teams, he enjoyed the good natured arguments which were the typical conversations that they both seemed to enjoy. The burly figure broke into a smile as he said, "Anthony, how are you?" Frank was the only one of Rocky's friends who called him the name from which his mother never had varied. Actually, the name formality was as close to wit as Frank would indulge in for the remainder of the visit, which, as always would be devoted to the seriously superficial.

After Rocky's pro forma response to Frank's greeting, the old collegiate teammates and scapegraces spent the next hour re-affirming their devotion to America's secular religion, professional football. Frank expatiated on the astuteness of his current favorite among professional football coaches. Rocky insistently attributed that particular team's success to a combination of luck and superior personnel rather than to coaching genius. Finding his tolerance of the subject less than when he was younger, Rocky changed the subject to the purpose behind his visit in advance of the reunion on Saturday, where there would be numerous conversations like the one he was having with Frank.

"You knew about Dave?" Rocky asked.

"Yeh, I heard when it happened," Frank said, shaking his head. After a brief silence, Frank added, "I never knew a nicer guy. And not a bad halfback, either. No Hall of Famer, but a pretty good running back."

"He was that," Rocky nodded. Frank and Rocky both having been linemen, the praise just uttered was normally as effusive as the two got about the position players they considered the beneficiaries of their harder labors.

Rocky smiled and said, "I remember your saying one time that you'd rather block for Dave than any of those other backs because you at least knew the ball was going somewhere if you made a good block."

"When didn't I ever make a good block, Anthony?" retorted Frank, frowning with mock gravity and addressing Rocky again with counterfeit formality. Rocky knew better than to take Frank's assertion as a serious boast.

"Oh, hell, how did I forget," Rocky sighed, feigning contrition. "You always made your block, provided I'd told you who you were supposed to block."

"I knew the plays," Frank insisted.

"Yeh, and I used to be six feet three and have shrunk to five nine." said Rocky.

"Six three or five nine," Frank retorted, "we'd have gone to the Tangerine Bowl if you'd have scored in that last game."

"Excuse the hell out of me, pal, but I've re-run that play in my mind a million times since then, and the guy catches me from behind every time. I can't seem to get my memory to increase my speed," said Rocky with a sigh.

"I don't see why you can't improve. Every reunion, when I talk to the rest of the guys, they seem to get better. The whole team gets better except for you. Two more reunions and we'll be national champs."

"Too bad Dave won't be around to enjoy it," said Rocky.

"Yeh, that is too bad. Frank picked up his empty coffee cup, stared at it for a moment and set it back down. "He was a great guy to be around. He'd do anything for you. You remember that time we were jailed for being drunk?"

"How could I forget it? We'd probably have been there longer than one night if our psych prof hadn't paid our fine."

"Naw," Frank shrugged. "I never told you. Afterward, Dave told me we didn't have to worry. He had collected the money from the guys to pay our fine, but the prof beat him to the justice of the peace."

"No kidding? I never heard that before."

Frank smiled. "I talked to some of the guys to thank them. They said that they hadn't had much money to contribute. The pot was mostly Dave's."

They lapsed into a thoughtful silence. Rocky mentally worked on the organization of the eulogy he was to deliver. As he was thinking that he should gather some information on Dave's career as a teacher and school administrator, Frank asked him how soon Beatrice was coming to pick him up. When he was told it would not be for two or three hours yet, Frank said, "Good. You can join me for my weekly lunch with Max Grossman."

"You lunch every week with Max Grossman?" Rocky queried with furrowed brow. Grossman was a mutual acquaintance from college who had been noted for his bizarre and unpredictable behavior, even beyond the standards of Rocky, Frank and their cohort. Grossman's fondness for embarrassing pranks and his careless appearance had won him the nickname Maximum Gross.

Frank's periodic reports to Rocky of Grossman's doings since his college days confirmed that Max had not changed. Frank admitted to amusement at Grossman's bizarre antics. Atkinson had once related to Rocky the time that Max had arrived to sit beside Frank in a diner. Max pretended to be a stranger who was approaching Frank in a state of despair at being penniless. In a monologue of stage whispers loud enough to be overheard by the stranger to their left, Max coaxed Frank to buy him a meal. Frank, cooperating in the act, refused rather brusquely and remained intransigent as Max persisted in his pleading. Finally the stranger beside them told Max to order what he wanted and he would pay the check. Max, who usually ordered rather frugally, ordered a full meal and played at effusive gratitude toward the man who paid his check. Frank explained to Rocky that saving a few dollars on a meal by trickery was perhaps the least miserly of Max's manipulations.

During the short drive to the restaurant, Frank told Rocky of the money saving manipulations to which Max resorted recently in having a woodland cabin constructed. Acting as his own contractor,

Max had not only negotiated for favorable prices on most of the materials, Max was also careful to insist that the materials were either cheap seconds or left over items garnered from careful scrutiny of personal ads. The few building materials Max had not been able to scrounge had been bought through wrangling negotiations that eventually made him persona non grata at the local building materials concern.

Of course the frugal acquisition of materials was profligate behavior compared to Max's acquiring a construction crew. Max had run down every hard-pressed illiterate of intermittent sobriety and set them to work at below minimum wage. Naturally, Max had to provide constant supervision for the construction to finish in anything close to adequate condition.

Max's material maulers had to redo several of the more bizarre features of their work, but at the wages Max paid, such duplication of work was not expensive. Even at that, Frank chuckled as he related the outcome. It was fortunate for Max that the remote rural location of the cabin was not subject to any sort of building codes or other requirements. The structure was neither weather-tight nor reliable in its water supply or electricity. Frank emphasized that Rocky should reject any invitation to spend an afternoon there.

By the time they reached the restaurant, Rocky silently wondered why Frank continued to be a close acquaintance of the manipulative and miserly Max. Rocky did not risk asking Frank why, and assumed that Frank continued the association for its entertainment value. The restaurant proved to be an unpretentious but bright and colorful place. Frank and Rocky selected a table near the back of the large square room.

Before long, the tall shambling figure of Max Grossman entered and began to walk toward them. He looked to Rocky not much different than the collegian of four decades previously. A sweat-stained baseball cap topped Max's egg-shaped head, which had escaped fleshiness despite the man's age. Max's quarter-moon smile that Rocky remembered from years ago was still in place, though one still had the same problem of understanding whether it was benevolent or malevolent. Rocky had concluded years ago, that the smile could be either friendly or malicious depending on whether the mercurial Max felt kindly or devious.

"The Rock himself," Max said, grinning and extending his hand in greeting.

"How are you, Max?" Rocky said and shook Grossman's hand firmly as Max dropped down into the chair opposite him. Rocky said, "Frank suggested that I join you two for lunch. I hope you don't mind."

"It's great, Rocky," Max assured. "What brings you here, all the way from California?"

"Well, you know there's the reunion Saturday." Rocky paused, unsure whether he might be injecting a sensitive subject. "I guess you don't go to those."

"I don't get invited," Max said with an air of coolness that signaled wounded feelings.

"Oh, don't pull any bullshit, Max," Frank Atkinson said. Turning to Rocky, he said, "You remember that years ago they took off the invitation list all those who had never showed for one of the events. That's why Max doesn't get an invitation. And a lot he gives a shit."

"It's Barbara's fault," Max grunted. "She never wanted to go."

"Come on, Max, that's not true and you know it," Frank said. "I heard her say myself that she would have been happy to go. She had friends who went regularly, you know damn well."

Max looked at Rocky and nodded toward Frank, "Frank thinks Barbara's a saint. Just like everyone else. Nobody knows what a bad time that woman has given me. Now she's left me and wants a divorce."

Rocky looked at Frank, who raised his hand as though to ward off a request that he comment. "That's too bad, Max," Rocky said. "I mean if you'd still like to keep things together. You have kids, I recollect."

Max nodded affirmatively. "Both in college now. She's turned them on me."

"Maybe your making them beg for tuition money has something to do with it, Max," Frank offered.

"I've always paid it," Max retorted, the grin on his face uninterpretable. Had he enjoyed the children's having to coax the money out of him? Or did he take satisfaction in supporting them? The waitress came to take their order, interrupting a conversation that Rocky was just as happy not to have continue.

Later, the trio was nearing the end of their meal when Max returned to the unwanted topic. "Still and all, Rocky, I'd rather we got back together than divorced." In view of his own martial uncertainty, Rocky remained silent. He looked at Frank and saw a surprised expression registering there. "Would you help me with that, Rocky?" Max asked. The perpetual grin had disappeared for an expression that actually looked pleading.

"What do you mean, Max?"

"Would you help me get back together with Barbara? I have a plan. I was going to ask Frank to help me, but I think that maybe someone who seems more like a detached outsider might give the plan a better chance of success with Barbara."

Rocky's impulse was to refuse. But if Max really wanted to save his marriage, it seemed small not to help if he could. "What is this plan of yours, Max?"

"Barbara has moved out, Rocky. She's living with a woman that she teaches with at the high school. She won't even talk to me. I've written a letter of apology, promising that things would be different if she came home. I've even got it with me," Max explained and pulled an envelope out of a pocket inside his jacket. "I wish you'd take it to her for me, Rock."

Rocky was slow to respond. "A letter seems kind of indirect, Max. Why don't you just go see her?"

"Don't you think I've tried?" Grossman asked. The seemingly perpetual quarter moon smile had turned over into a mournful expression. "She won't see me. I don't know if she'll even read my letter, but it's my only chance, especially it you take it to her and coax her to read it."

Rocky looked at Frank, who was holding his empty coffee cup and looking to see if another swallow of coffee would magically appear in it. "Wouldn't it be better to have Frank do it? He's been friends with you and Barb for years. I haven't seen Barb since college. She may not even remember me."

"Of course she remembers you. It hasn't been too many years since the alumni magazine did that story on you with a picture and everything."

"Frank," Rocky began, "you've always gotten along with Barb, haven't you?"

"I think so, Rocky, and my wife Marcie is closer to her than almost anyone else, but Barb won't discuss Max or the marriage with us," Frank explained. Rocky studied Frank's face. He wondered if Frank was going along in some game Max was playing. He detected no signs of mischievousness in either man.

"Come on, Rocky, help me out here," Grossman pleaded. "You don't know what it's like to be breaking up after all these years."

Rocky was tempted to say that as a matter of fact he did. He wondered if he should counsel Max that he ought to leave well enough alone. Yet he felt a tug of obligation as well. "All I've got to do is give her the letter and ask her to read it, right?"

Max nodded earnestly. "Just tell her what it is and take your best shot at asking her to read it."

"You don't think she'll get emotional, do you?"

"You know how controlled she was in college," Max offered. "She hasn't changed."

Rocky reluctantly assented to delivering the letter, hoping that Barb would not be found at home and he would avoid the burdensome task. Frank drove the three of them in his car to where Betsy was living with her teaching colleague. Frank parked some distance from the house to which Rocky was directed. Rocky approached the dwelling reluctantly, despite it being the most attractive house and yard on an altogether well-kept and prosperous looking row of properties. Rocky paused a few seconds before he pressed the doorbell. A response was long enough in coming that his hopes had risen that no one was at home. However, eventually a tall, dark-haired woman, with plain facial features but well-groomed in overall appearance stood before him behind the screen door and peered at him. "Yes?" she asked blandly.

"Hello," Rocky began, "I am looking for Barbara Grossman. I understand that she lives here."

"She does," nodded the woman. "May I ask who wants to see her."

"My name is Tony Rocco. I knew her years ago in college. I'm collecting some information for a reunion of some of mutual college acquaintances this Saturday, and I was hoping to speak with her regarding that, " Rocky said. He felt justified in his indirect approach for fear that the woman would offer to deliver the letter, and he would further complicate the situation by insisting on seeing Barbara. He suspected that the direct revelation of why he was there would get him turned away without seeing Barb. That would probably be a blessing, but he owed Max some degree of diligence.

The woman opened the screen door and invited him in. "She's out back doing some gardening. Please follow me and I'll take you to her." They walked down a hallway that led directly out on to a porch and down a few steps into a well-tended yard that was surrounded by a privet hedge which served as a backdrop for a border of flowers that added a multi-colored gaiety to the lush green of grass and hedge. "Someone to see you, Barb," said Rocky's guide to the kneeling figure working in the farthest reach of the flowering border.

As the woman got to her feet, she was easily recognizable to Rocky as the college student of four decades ago. Barbara had remained as slender as she had been then. Under the broad brim of the straw hat that shaded her face, the same horn-rimmed glasses contrasted starkly with the familiar milk-white complexion. Of course, a few faint wrinkles deepened as she smiled fainted at Rocky's approach. "Tony Rocco," Barb said, "my heavens, it's been decades since I've seen you."

"I wasn't sure that you'd remember me, Barb."

"Oh, Tony, between the alumni newsletter and Frank Atkinson's periodic reports, it's not likely I'd forget. How are you?"

"Fine, Barb."

"Claire," Barb smiled to the woman who had brought Tony along, "this is Tony Rocco, a college classmate of mine."

"He did introduce himself, Barbara. Why don't you two sit in the shade, and I'll bring you some lemonade and let you visit," she offered and motioned toward some chairs under an umbrella-topped table nearby.

After they sat, Tony answered Barb's inquiry about Beatrice at some length. Claire brought the lemonade and excused herself to look after some chore. Rocky told Barbara of he efforts to collect impressions from old friends for use in Dave Christiansen's eulogy. Not surprisingly, Barbara had little personal reminisce to contribute since she and Max had had no contact with Dave, who worked in another school district, since college. However, she did report with pride that Dave had been held in high esteem in public school education circles in the region as a rational and effective administrator. As her memories of college days were awakened, Barbara expressed the platonic affection that was universally felt by Dave's female collegiate contemporaries.

"Truthfully, Barb, I didn't really expect you'd have anything different to say than what I've already got. I actually had another reason for visiting with you today."

"What was that, Tony?" Barbara asked, her gentle voice seeming to Rocky to have a firmness he was glad to hear despite the drastic changes occurring in her life.

"I saw Max today," Rocky said. She frowned slightly but continued to look at Rocky blandly. "He told me about the breakup. He seems very sorry about it, Barb. He says that you refuse to see him. So he asked me do deliver his written apology to you." Rocky pulled the letter from his pocket and extended it toward Barbara.

Barb looked at Rocky with an expression of dismay. She was obviously upset at Rocky's offering the envelope. She stared for some time at the envelope as though it were an explosive before she shook her head and said coldly, "I really don't care to read it; thank you, Tony."

"I didn't expect you to feel so adamant, Barb. "Don't you want to even try to reconcile?"

"You have no idea how long and how hard I tried to make my marriage work, Tony. I--in fact, we—are beyond trying any more. I'll never let anyone treat me again like Max did."

"Surely he wasn't abusive."

Barb shook her head with an air of sadness. "If you mean physical abuse. That isn't Max's style, but he was nevertheless abusive."

Rocky shook his head. "That doesn't sound like Max."

Barb said, "There's no other word for it but abuse, not that he ever laid a hand on me. Max is domineering, unpredictable, selfish, and cruel."

Rocky frowned uncertainly. "Max always had a bizarre sense of humor. Surely you knew that when you married him."

"For thinking he'd soon grow out of that, I'm partly responsible for what he put me through." She paused a moment. "I'll take that back. He did grow out of it. Continued past a certain point, that quirky humor becomes cruel. Eventually it will shred your soul.

"And he never puts a disagreement behind him. Worse yet, long after you think a disagreement has past, you'll be the target of one of his cruel pranks meant to even the score for the imagined wrong that he thinks he's suffered. Believe me, his so-called sense of humor has lost all its charm."

Rocky frowned in puzzled disbelief. Barb sensed his conflicted state and smiled for the first time. She took the envelope from Rocky's hand and tore open the envelope. After a glance at the sheet of paper she took out, she handed it to Rocky and said, "You read the latest of his heartfelt apologies."

Rocky examined the paper and read what was obviously the annual tax statement for a residential property that was in Max's name. Now embarrassed that he had been the bearer of such a message, Rocky mumbled a contrite apology to Barbara.

His contrition brought another smile from Barb. "Live with that sense of humor for almost forty years and then tell me what you think of Max Grossman. You probably don't remember, but his nickname in college was Maximum Gross. Never was a nickname more appropriate."

Rocky interrupted when Barb paused in her cathartic assertion and said, "I remember the nickname, and I'm sorry if it turned out to be all too true. It's unfortunately too common for a spouse to be insensitive to a mate's feelings."

Rocky thought of his own marital situation. There wasn't a molecule of similarity between Max and his wife Beatrice; however, he was thinking of his own situation when he said, "The older I get, the more I think that what a couple need more than anything else in their relationship is kindness." He spoke to himself more than to Barb when he offered, "I'm sorry if that's gone from your marriage."

"It isn't gone, Tony. It was never there. You know what was the last straw. Without a word to me, Max took the money I had saved to help my parents move to the climate my father needed to help with his asthma and built himself a hideaway cabin in the woods."

Rocky had been told about Max's project, but the source of the funding was new information. He was momentarily appalled. Then he reasoned that if the Max Grossman of his college days had continued throughout his adulthood, the action was not really surprising. When he was given the envelope to deliver to Barb, Rocky thought it the case that Max was truly contrite. Rocky concluded that, having committed such an horrendous betrayal, he now saw the error of his ways. He agreed to Max's request because he felt Max needed a friend's help.

"What Max did was truly terrible, Barb. But don't you think there's a chance that, having now reached the depths of insensitivity, Max might one day see the error of his ways and change? Barb studied Rocky with a sad smile for a few moments before she answered. She said, "Tony, there was a time when something like this," she paused and took the tax bill Max had sent from Rocky's hand and crumpled it in her fist, "would have devastated me, but not any more. That's why I'm not angry with you for bringing it. I knew you hadn't read it or you'd have refused to bring it."

Rocky responded with a relieved chuckle. "Wow, Barb, you really don't register very high on the hostility index compared to what I'd be feeling in your place." Rocky reached for the paper she had crumpled into a sphere the size of a golf ball. "Let me take the tax bill back to the fool so he can pay his taxes. That will at least give me a pleasure."

Barb put the paper in her jeans. "Don't bother, Tony, This is undoubtedly a copy. Max is cruel, but he's not stupid."

Rocky shook he head in astonishment. "So a cruel prank is not a rarity with Max?"

"Do you know what Max wrote me when he got the notice that I'd filed for divorce? He said that if I did not drop my suit for divorce, He would assert to his attorney and publicly that I was having a lesbian relationship with Clair McKinley, the woman with whom I'm now living. That the assertion is not true, Max warned, would not prevent gossip from circulating and might well endanger both mine and Clair's jobs as teachers.

Rocky's face burned with embarrassment. "Barb, I am truly embarrassed, if I'd known what Max had really written, I'd never have brought it to you. I believed him when told me he was asking your forgiveness because he wanted you back."

"Rocky, believe me I'm not annoyed with you in the least. You just joined Victims of Max Grossman, the Evil Humorist. It's a pretty big club. But there's no long term liability from being a member once you've been a victim a few times."

"I admire your forbearance, Barb," Rocky said.

"You'll feel the same way when you realize he's harmless. Clair and I did nothing about his threat to out us as lesbians. He did nothing. Once he's gotten his jollies out of a jab he never follows through."

"So he never went through with his threat? And you're sure he won't in the future?" Rocky asked with furrowed brow.

Barb smiled, "He's a putz, Tony."

"Of course, where I come from, a rumor like that wouldn't raise an eyebrow, though it might get you hit on once in a while. But my guess is that around here it might cause a major stir."

Barb broadened her smile. "I'd pay money to see Clair get hit on. She's so straight she changed churches when hers got a woman minister.

Actually, Tony, in my case, Max just happened to raise my curiosity, and I find I could go either way. Clair accepts that I'm experimental and I try not to upset her by putting my new friends in proximity with her."

"And if Max finds out?" Rocky asked.

"I decided that I wouldn't deny it if anyone asked. If it bothers anyone, I'll just have to accept whatever they do or don't do about it, but they better be on firm legal ground."

Rocky could not suppress a smile. "Max may be in for a surprise some day."

"I'm beyond caring what he thinks. I'm sad that our kids think so ill of their father. I'm amazed that they still retain some affection for him underneath their anger. He was so unkind to them, Tony, but they're good kids making their way in the world. I wouldn't be surprised that Max thinks that the way he treated them has been the making of them. He's a fool if he does."

"He's a fool about more than that, Barb. I'm really sorry that I've been a party to one of his stupid pranks. I hope you'll forgive me." Rocky got to his feet and prepared to make his embarrassed retreat, grateful that his unwitting involvement in Max's unkind maneuver had not proven more unpleasant. "I hope you won't mind if tell him that I think it's time he stopped harassing you."

"Anything you say would only encourage him, Tony," Barb said as she stood and patted his arm gently. "If Max makes what he thinks is his devastating announcement about my life style, he'll just facilitate my going public without bother. I've been wondering how to do it myself without taking an activist position."

Rocky grinned as a thought struck him. "If you want, I can give him a hearty shove toward spreading the word."

"Sounds like you would like to beat the devil at his own game," said Barb, her eyes sparkling with the prospect of a joy that Rocky suspected came much too rarely.

"I'll admit to feeling a bit evil," Rocky said. "I suppose I should resist the temptation." Taking Barb's hands in his, he said, "Notwithstanding the absurdity of why I've come, Barb, I'm glad to have seen you. I'm sure Treece would have wanted to be along if she'd known I'd be seeing you."

"How is Beatrice, Tony? I hope things are well with you two." Barb asked earnestly.

Rocky sensed that the instant circumstances were not appropriate for either candor or intimate revelation. "She's fine. I'll tell her you asked." With that, Rocky smiled again at Barb and made his way around the side of the house and down the block to where Frank and Max waited in Frank's car.

Rocky approached the car and worked his face into the most placid unexpressive expression that he could muster. He slipped into the front passenger seat and said to Frank, "We'd better get going. Beatrice is supposed to be back to pick me up in about fifteen minutes."

They rode along silently for a few minutes, Rocky wondering how long Max would be able to maintain his silence. Finally, Max leaned forward and placed his forearms on the back of the front seat. "Did you give her the letter, Rock?"

"Yeh," Rocky nodded. If Max was expecting more, Rocky was not about to offer it.

"Did she read it?"

"Of course," Rocky said. Rocky saw Frank's curious sidewise glance. He seemed puzzled at Rocky's taciturnity.

There was another interlude of silence before Max whined, "Well, did she say anything?"

Rocky continued to face forward and said off-handedly. "Of course she did."

"Well for Christ's sake, what did she say?"

"Well, Max, I really didn't understand it," Rocky sighed, making a maximum effort at seeming puzzled.

"What do you mean, you didn't understand?" Max grumbled with growing impatience.

"Just that, I didn't understand." Rocky noted that Frank looked interested and was smiling at Max's impatience.

"What the hell did she say, Rocky? Max grumbled.

"She said 'well, this is unexpected'."

"No shit," Max wondered, "that's what she said?" Max asked leaning toward Rocky, looking confused. "Was she pissed off?"

"No," Rocky answered. "Calm as a baby taking its bottle. You must have written one hell of an apology, pal."

Max gasped in surprise. "Didn't she tell you what was in my letter?"

Rocky turned to look at Max. "Now why the hell would she tell me personal stuff like that?"

"And that's all she said?"

"I remember one other thing," Rocky said, but stopped at that.

"Well, shit, aren't you going to tell me."

Rocky shook his head from side to side in feigned perplexity. "I can't say I knew what she meant, but she must be feeling a lot more kindly toward you, old buddy."

"Hell, Rocky," Max muttered, "try not to be such a fountain of information. What did she say?"

Rocky fixed his gaze forward and said, "She said that it looked like you'd be making things a lot simpler for her from now on."

Max leaned back in his seat resignedly. "And she wasn't pissed or anything?"

"Not a bit, buddy," Rocky assured Max. "You really pulled it off this time. My hat's off to you."

They finished the rest of the ride in silence. Frank Atkinson's furrowed brow and faint smile at the situation led Rocky to conclude that he knew nothing of the contents of Max's note to Barbara. It pleased Rocky that his old friend was unaware of Max's cruel joke.

Rocky was delighted to see as they approached Atkinson's home that Beatrice was waiting for him. He was anxious to escape the morning's bizarre activities.

Chapter 5

Beatrice had not only had a pleasant visit with her cousin, but had also, with the cousin's help, managed to arrange a family picnic for the day after tomorrow. Rocky was not upset by the news. There were among Beatrice's numerous relatives, many that he found pleasant enough to be around for a day. However, he realized that he had so far garnered little in the way of reminiscences about Dave Christiansen to add many people's sentiments to the eulogy he would be delivering four days hence.

After considering time, logistics and people's intimacy of acquaintance with Dave since college days, he decided to look up Tank Robb, a teammate of Dave's and Rocky's who had subsequently spent his entire teaching career in the high school where Dave had been appointed in mid-career as assistant principal and later principal. If that possible contact failed or ended early, he noted that a second contemporary during their college days lived not greatly distant from Tank Robb and might also be visited. He would have the car, since Beatrice wanted to be dropped off at the home of the cousin she had visited that day to plan the family reunion picnic two days hence.

After taking Beatrice to her cousin's home the next morning, Rocky armed himself with an address from their alma mater's alumni directory and an area map and proceeded toward Tank Robb's address. Several only slightly contradictory driving directions later from one gas station attendant and a succession of passersby, Rocky paused once again at an intersection to study a pair of puzzling street signs.

A passerby who noted his perplexity informed him that the home of Coach Robb, who was known to all in the town, was nearby.

Soon Rocky was ringing the bell at the home with the address he had for the man who had been the star running back of his and Dave Christiansen's college football team. He was about to give up on a response when the door opened and the space was immediately filled with a wide thick body that was a larger thicker-waisted version of the one that had made Tank Robb an effective power running back in his youth.

"Tank," Rocky smiled and said, "you haven't shrunk since you graduated from college."

A tanned face that had added only a little puffiness to the square outline of years ago peered back at Rocky and struggled to recognize his visitor. Lifting his chin in accompaniment of a grunt of recognition, Tank said, "Tony Rocco, the biggest bullshitter who ever played a football game. What the hell are you doing here?"

"I came to see you, Tank," Rocky answered with mock gravity. "I here you've lost your appetite and the processed food industry is worried about its profits, especially the beer and potato chips people."

"You don't look like any ad for a fitness place yourself, you stupid wop."

"I'm going to start cutting down as soon as I get back home, Tank."

"Yeh, and I've got a closet full of size 46 sport coats I'm just about to get back into next week," said Robb as he patted his ample waistline. "What brings you to these parts? Last I heard you lived in California."

"That's where I live," Rocky answered. "I'm here for the old jocks reunion this Saturday. You're going aren't you?"

With sudden disgust in his tone, Robb grumbled, "You're not here to coax me to go to that crap, are you?"

"That's not the reason I'm here, Tank," Rocky answered, sensing the need to be conciliatory, "but I'm curious about why you're so turned off by the reunion."

"It's a long story."

"I'd love to hear it after I take care of the matter I've come about. Do you have time to talk?"

"I have to pick up my wife at the golf course in about an hour. I guess we can talk for a few minutes," said Tank as he stepped aside so that Rocky could enter.

When they were settled in a pleasant living room, Rocky perched on the forward edge of a couch seat, and Tank dropped into a leather chair that showed signs of being his favorite. Rocky said, "I'd better get right to the point since you're short of time. You have surely heard about Dave Christiansen's dying over a year ago. I've been asked to give a eulogy of him at the reunion. I've been visiting some of his college friends and former teammates this week to collect their sentiments for use in the eulogy. You worked with him during the administrator part of his career for about twenty-five years, I understand. I'd be interested in your thoughts about Dave for the eulogy."

Tank stiffened in his chair and stared silently at Rocky for a long time. Finally he said, "Did you come just to piss me off, Rocco?"

"What do you mean?" asked Rocky, truly mystified.

"You ever seen me at one of those stupid reunions?" Tank asked contemptuously.

Rocky searched his memory. "Yes. A long time ago. In fact, the first couple, if I remember right."

"Right. By then I had had enough of The Dave Christiansen Show."

"Wait," Rocky nodded as his memory was awakened. "Come to think of it, why you haven't been at the more recent reunion is always referred to briefly in some vague way that's never been clear to me."

"I don't need to sit around and try to imagine myself a good football player. I was a good football player, a damn good football player."

"I never heard anyone say otherwise, Tank. Back then, none of us ever doubted that it was you who made us winners. Our memories are clear on that, at least. But surely you can't be upset by the harmless exaggerations of someone else's contribution to games long past, can you, Tank? Dave was such a good guy in so many ways that his image was bound to be exaggerated. Nobody's really kidding themselves about who made our team successful."

Rocky smiled at a recollection that now came. "Frank Atkinson says that two more reunions and we'll become division two national champions."

"I don't like to talk about football, so I don't go. Let it go at that, O.K.?"

Rocky remembered that, one of the recurring topics of discussion when he and his former teammates discussed what their college friends had done with their lives since college, the mystery of Tank Robb having abandoned his football coaching career at the very height of his success was always mentioned but never explained.

Rocky looked at his stellar teammate of years ago earnestly. "Tank, you must have your reasons for not wanting to talk football. And I have no doubt that if you came to the reunion that you'd be asked a million times why you stopped coaching so suddenly. You resigned a week after your team won the state high school championship, as I recall. Just tell the guys you don't want to talk about it. They'll respect that."

"The guys," Tank grumbled with a shake of his head. "You think I want to see the guys?"

"Tank, I think you're forgetting that you have a lot of friends who'll be at that reunion," Rocky said resignedly. "However, I respect your feelings if you don't want to come to the reunion, but you might still want to give me some thoughts for my eulogy of Dave. You probably knew him better than any of us. You worked at the same high school for more than twenty-five years, didn't you?"

"We worked in the same building for twenty-seven years. I never talked to him for the last twenty of those years. Wouldn't talk to him today if I passed him on the street."

Rocky frowned disbelievingly. "Tank. He was your building principal for the last fifteen of those years. Surely the two of you had to talk to each other."

"Oh, he talked, but he knew better than to expect me to answer."

"You didn't talk to your boss for fifteen years?" Rocky asked. He was more curious than shocked. Rocky's own lifetime career in education teaching from junior high school through the doctoral level had convinced him that no absurdity of human conduct was beyond the realm of probability in the academic world.

Tank shrugged unconcernedly, "Who needed to talk? Hey, I can read memos. You think because I taught phys ed and driver training that I can't read?"

"I believe you can read, Tank. It's just that, in most professions, refusing to talk to your boss would be a basis for discipline."

"What could the prick do to me when he was principal? He'd already done the worst that he could do before he became principal."

"Tank," Rocky sighed and looked aslant at the chilly face of his old acquaintance. "Dave Christiansen? The most humane, forgiving guy that the rest of us ever knew; he screwed you over?"

"You're shocked," Tank grimaced. He shook his head in disgust. "You're just like the rest of them, transforming their adolescent admiration into full scale worship over the years during those bullshit reunions."

"You exaggerate, Tank. It's true that Dave was always respected. And everyone else but you seems to think he was an unusually fine school administrator."

"He fooled a lot of people who didn't know what he was really like," Tank snorted dismissively.

Rocky's expression showed how dubious he found Tank's assertions. He was not certain that his attitude toward Tank Robb was entirely fair. Years ago he had admired Tank's prowess as a football running back. However, he had never found his teammate companionable. Not many did. Tank's aggressiveness was not left on the playing field. His pride occasionally slipped into arrogance. While Tank was normally accorded the deference that his stardom merited in a context of fanaticism for athletics, the powerful running back was quick to remind someone if he felt his importance was being ignored.

"O.K., Tank," Rocky challenged, "you tell me: you tell me what Dave Christiansen was really like."

"I don't want to go into it," Tank responded with a warding off wave of his arm. The huge hand and sapling-sized arm had not shrunk from the weapon that had knocked off many a potential tackler who approached the Tank too high when he was under a full head of steam. "I'll just say that Dave Christiansen was not the saint that you guys thought he'd become since college."

"You sure you don't just begrudge him his success, Tank?" Rocky asked with some defensiveness. He did count himself among those who thought Christiansen had been a man of unusual integrity and goodness.

"His success, huh? His success? You know who made him a success? You know how he got to be a principal? By getting me fired from my coaching job. That's how. You think that it's a coincidence he became a principal the fall after I stopped coaching?"

Rocky responded candidly. "I have no idea why you stopped coaching. I don't think anyone else does either. The question inevitably comes up every time the group gets together, but no one ever claims to know."

Tank was silent for a long time, perhaps wrestling with telling what he had been loathe to reveal until now. "When I gave up coaching, I said the usual bullshit about wanting to spend more time with my family and doing more teaching, but the truth is, if I hadn't resigned, they were going to fire me. Fire me. A month after I got Chestnut Ridge High School the only state football championship it has ever gotten, not to mention the three consecutive league titles that led up to that championship season."

Rocky was quick to respond. "Dave was just an assistant principal at the time. How could he possibly have had anything to do with your being forced out?"

"There were people on the board who thought the football program was being over-emphasized. They were looking for a reason to get me. Dave Christiansen gave the board some damaging information about the program that I had nothing to do with and made me the fall guy. The board forced me out. And what do you know," Tank continued, gesturing like a magician bringing his slight of hand to a successful conclusion, "the principal retired the following spring; and guess was chosen principal for the coming fall? Good Old Dave. He sold me out to get that job. He advanced his career by being smooth and slippery and that's the way he stayed. So don't tell me what a saint he was as a school principal. I paid with my career for him to get there to begin his saintly career."

Rocky couldn't ignore Tank's bitterness. "You won't care to be specific, would you? What was this damaging information that you had nothing to do with?"

"Some teacher was late turning in her grades. It was a set of grades that included one that would have made my star running back ineligible before the state championship game. The assistant principal, Saint Dave, was responsible for checking eligibility. He informed the principal and the board of the circumstances that had made it possible for the kid to play. The board wouldn't believe that I didn't know about the kid's grade. They decided to hush the whole thing rather than forfeit the championship if I resigned. The whole thing wouldn't have been noticed if Christiansen had just let the situation pass unnoticed. But no; he was more interested in giving his career a boost."

For a while, Rocky continued to argue with Tank about whether or not Dave had had any choice to do other than what he had done. He found Tank Robb as bullish in his beliefs as he had been in his running style. Changing the subject, Rocky renewed his urging that Tank come to the reunion. He pointed out to Tank that there were many who would be at the reunion who had not seen him in decades and would enjoy seeing him. Finally, he accepted Tank's immovability and took his leave.

Chapter 6

Rocky's thoughts were in turmoil as he drove away from the residence of Tank Robb. His life-long regard for Dave Christiansen and the absence of any feeling of friendliness toward his former star teammate inclined him to disbelieve Robb's damning allegations against the icon he was preparing to eulogize in a few days. On the other hand, he wondered if he was cherishing an illusion of that did not exist. Having lived a complicated professional and personal life, Rocky was no longer surprised that people's behavior conflicted with their reputations. He had seen surprising goodness as well as unexpected baseness in people whose reputations varied greatly from what they did.

It was possible that others in close contact with Dave besides Tank knew a Dave Christiansen who was not the admirable person perceived by his college friends living at great distances who enjoyed a social interlude with him on rare occasions absent professional requirements and stress. With typical modesty Dave never spoke of his professional success. His friends knew what articles in the university's alumni newsletter said of him and tales that were repeated second and third hand of his fairness, humanity and wisdom in the performance of his duties and in his nurturing of his family.

Rocky wondered if he was stubbornly refusing to recognize the imperfections of the man he had always viewed as one of the rare exceptions to the human tendency to sacrifice integrity to gain success. He felt as he did at the times when he needed to remove a bitter taste from his mouth by eating something pleasant. He had planned, if time permitted, to visit with a pair college acquaintances who would most likely not add anything new for the eulogy but would be pleasant to visit. Richie and Marty Havens had married shortly after graduation and, according to his information, lived in the same town as Tank. They would be a welcome antidote to talking to Tank, he expected.

Rocky did not have an address for the Havenses. He spotted a restaurant. If it had a public phone and a local directory, he should have no trouble getting an address for the couple. There was, it turned out, a directory; however, he could find no listing for the Havenses. Slightly dispirited, Rocky considered how next to proceed. He decided that a mid-morning snack and a cup of coffee would be both a needed diversion and a chance to think. As he munched at an oversized muffin and sipped his coffee he spotted an abandoned copy of a newspaper on the next table. For want of nothing better to do, he appropriated it and leafed through it with no particular intent. The sports page caught his eye and from long habit he began to look for the previous day's major league baseball scores. Then a feature column with the columnist's picture beside the heading caught his eye. The face in the small rectangle looked familiar; however, the general appearance looked a little too youthful for it to be anyone Rocky might have known in the past. Beside the picture, the column was headed WRIGHT ON SPORTS. The combination of the name in the heading and the face in picture connected for Rocky. The journalist appeared to be a younger version of another of his college acquaintances, Brad Wright. Wright had not been an athlete other than for his enthusiastic participation in intramurals; however, he loved sports fanatically. He had been singlehandedly the student newspaper's sports editor-columnist, sports reporter and photographer. Brad had, like a number of his college contemporaries, become a teacher. Unfortunately, he had died at an early age of cancer. A brief further examination of the little photo convinced Rocky that the journalist was quite likely the son of the Brad Wright who had gone to college with him.

While Rocky finished his coffee, he considered that it might be pleasant to meet the son who looked so much like his father and to discuss with him how it felt to do professionally what his father had done so enthusiastically as an amateur. Rocky recognized that his desire to meet the journalist was motivated by more than to tell the man of his acquaintance with his father. If this Brad Wright had been in his present job for some considerable length of time, he might know something about Tank Robb's allegations against Dave Christiansen. Why not, reasoned Rocky, talk to the man and see if he could confirm or contradict Tank Robb's allegations about the role that Dave Christiansen had played in the ending of Tank's football coaching career. Rocky hastened to the phone directory to call the newspaper and try to get a meeting with the sportswriter Brad Wright.

A half hour later, Rocky was making his way through a cluttered newsroom where he had been directed toward the back of a large room full of cubicles separated by five-foot high dividers. In a corner cubicle sat a middle aged man who looked very much like what Rocky's college acquaintance would have looked like at the age of the man who now looked up and smiled at Rocky.

"Mr. Rocco?" the journalist asked as he rose to shake hands. "I'm Brad Wright."

"I'm glad to meet you, Mr. Wright. Please call me 'Tony', or, 'Rocky', if you wish."

"I'd be delighted to call you 'Rocky'. Please sit down." Wright gestured toward the chair beside his desk and re-settled himself in the chair behind the desk. Wright grinned at Rocky and said, "You know, this is something of a treat. Having one of the story time characters of my youth come to life." Seeing Rocky's puzzled expression, Wright continued. "My dad used to tell me Rocky Rocco stories when we'd get to talking about sports. Were you as tough and undisciplined as a football player as my father made you out?"

Rocky had to laugh. "Tough? That's debatable. But undisciplined? That's for sure. Your dad was always charitable about my shennigans."

"You're nowhere near as big as I expected you to be."

Rocky shook his head as he continued to grin. "As a veteran sportswriter, you know how football players get bigger and better with age. You guys in the business are major contributors. I sure as hell didn't have either size or speed. One of our coaches said that he could time me with a calendar. Enthusiasm and abandon, those probably made me look a little bigger than I actually was. Of course, no one was of the size that college players are today. I suppose most of us from then would get cut from the team today as undersized."

"I refuse to even consider that. I prefer to preserve my childhood illusions," said Brad. Rocky could not help thinking how much the younger Wright's easy smile and animated face were like his father's. It brought back memories of a lanky friend whose skinny body denied him the opportunity to play intercollegiate sports and who compensated for his loss by applying his sharp mind and intimate knowledge of games to writing about them.

"Everyone who knew your father in college was saddened when you and your mother lost him so soon," Rocky said sincerely. "A lot of us who knew and admired him have kept in touch by a getting together every few years. Your dad is always remembered with fondness."

"Thank you for saying that. I was pretty young when he died. I wish I had gotten to have him around longer." Looking away from Rocky, Wright reflected silently for a while, then brightened and looked back at his visitor. "What brings you to these parts? I'm guessing that you live some distance from here."

"California, actually," Rocky said. "We're having a reunion of the old group of college friends and their spouses this Saturday. As it happens, the man who began our reunions, actually the most admired and loved of our group, has died recently. I've been assigned to deliver a eulogy of him. So I've been spending a few days gathering reminiscences and impressions from old friends to use in my eulogy."

Wright nodded. "Dave Christiansen, right?"

"You knew him?" Rocky asked hopefully.

"Not personally. But he was kind of a legend among people in the region as the best school administrator around. Among other things, he maintained that balancing of athletic support and academic standards in a way that the public admired. But other than what I've just said, which I'm sure you've already gotten from other people, I can't tell you of anything that would be useful to you."

"Actually, there may be something you can help me get an accurate account of," Rocky said hopefully.

"I can't imagine what it would be, but I'll help if I can," offered Brad.

"Were you writing sports for this paper when Tank Robb gave up coaching?" Rocky asked.

Wright's wry smile was identical to Rocky's recollection of the middle-aged man's father.

"I have a hunch that you've just visited with Mr. Robb."

Rocky returned the smile in kind. "And I have a hunch that you are familiar with the story."

"More than one version, actually. Is there any particular one you'd like to hear?"

"I think your version is the one I'd prefer."

Wright settled back in his chair and appeared to be collecting his thoughts. "I'd been writing sports for eight or nine years at the time. Writing about local high school football was the easiest part of the job then. Maybe you remember how fanatically interested people in this part of the state are about football, particularly high school football. The paper will get a flood of letters for a coupe months even on something so inconsequential as people not liking the local high school's new uniforms

"And when the local team is winning, anything and everything about it fascinates the readers. The enthusiasm is intense when the team takes the league championship, but, if they continue winning in the playoffs, nothing else is talked of until the trauma of a loss in the playoffs. At one of those times when a school has a run of good players, making the playoffs becomes a routine expectation. Then, if there is the occurrence of a rarity, a state championship, the town collectively experiences nirvana. A sportswriter's only problem then is finding enough superlatives to ladle on everything from the kids to the coaching."

Wright leaned forward in his chair for emphasis. "And I assure you, I didn't have to fake it when Tank Robb's team had a state title season. The kids were really good. There was tremendous talent on that team. You name it: size, speed, passing and kicking skill, defense--everything. Robb's offense and defense seemed nothing short of perfection.

"So you can imagine what a shocker it was when an anonymous letter arrives in the editor's office a week after the team won the state championship saying that Coach Robb was being forced out although it would be publicly announced that he was choosing to step down. I still remember the editor handing me the letter and telling me to look into it as discretely as I could."

Rocky nodded knowingly. "Your editor had a lot of faith in you. I grew up in this part of the state. The sudden resignation of a coach who'd won a state championship would be a bigger deal than a leak at a nuclear power plant."

"In fact, there was one about that time at Three Mile Island," Wright said with a shake of his head. "We gave more space to the Robb resignation than we did to the Three Mile Island nuclear power plant leak. Apparently, you haven't forgotten the importance of football in the land of your youth."

"You're going to tell me about your investigation, I hope," Rocky beseeched.

"I will, as long as we understand that I wouldn't want to be cited as a source." Brad shrugged his shoulders in a gesture of resignation. "I can't document what is the obvious truth of the matter and the only person involved who is still alive neither admits to the truth nor would sit still for allegations regarding which I have no confirmation."

Rocky affirmed his intention to respect Brad Wright's request for confidentiality about the story.

Satisfied with Rocky's promise, Brad Wright began his account. "Following up on the anonymous letter, I called Coach Robb and asked for an interview. Even though he had refused to talk to anyone about his resignation since issuing his statement, he readily agreed to an interview.

"I was puzzled when he received me so cordially in the office he was about to vacate. He had always be a hostile interviewee, despite what had over the years been uniformly favorable press. He was usually defensive and closemouthed, always anticipating that he wasn't going to receive fair treatment in whatever was written. I asked him why he was making this striking exception in his refusal to grant interviews or even hold conversations with friends on this subject.

"It had occurred to me that he himself might be the author of the anonymous letter asserting that his resignation wasn't voluntary. He wouldn't be the first person to try to arouse public sentiment to reverse a decision adverse to him that he thought was unfair.

"Wearing the blandest expression I had seen on him in the nearly ten years I'd interviewed him about his team, Robb said, 'I've never turned you down for an interview. Hell, I went to college with your father. I knew and liked him. We were friends. I couldn't turn you down for an interview even now.'

"The expression on your face confirms my inference that Robb hadn't been a friend of my father in college. That's no surprise. If his interpersonal approach was then what it has been since, my father wouldn't have cared for him.

"I expressed my appreciation for the unique opportunity. I began by saying, 'Coach, I realize this is a trying time for you, so I'll get right to the point. The newspaper has received an anonymous letter asserting that your resignation was not voluntary, but that you actually are being forced out. Is there any truth to that?'

"Robb stared at me with an expression of unusual tranquility for him. I had been prepared for an explosive reaction from him. I remember once I had asked him if he had second thoughts about a play-calling decision that didn't work out and got five minutes of bluster that didn't go near answering my question.

"'I don't have any comment on that,'" he said.

"So you won't say the letter's untrue? I asked, trying the standard reporter's ploy of putting words into the mouth of a source who refused to comment. Robb's tranquil deportment was unchanged. 'I didn't say anything,' he said, maintaining his bland expression. I had expected a self-serving hint intended to let the cat out of the bag without violating any promise of confidentiality he'd made to the board. Neither was there an expression of outrage at an attempt to maneuver him.

"I asserted, 'Coach, you've got to admit, your resignation comes in very mysterious circumstances, unless you have a health problem you're not at liberty to disclose. You are a relatively young man.

You're at the pinnacle of high school coaching success: a string of league titles followed by a state championship. An announcement that you were moving into the college ranks seems a lot more likely than one that you are giving up coaching.'

"'My health is fine,'" he said. "'and I'm not changing jobs.'"

"I was struggling against his uninformative terseness. 'You seem to enjoy coaching more than anyone else I've ever interviewed.'

"'I have enjoyed it. It's been my life.'"

"And yet you're giving it up. Surely you can see why the anonymous letter seems a plausible explanation.

"'I won't comment on the letter. You make sure of that; if you write a story, you make that clear. No comment on the letter or on my resignation for that matter.'

"Spending further time with him seemed pointless. As much as for a means of closure than for pursuing the story, I asked him, 'Do you mind if I talk to Mr. Baxter, the principal about this?'" The expression on Robb's face revealed for just an instant that I'd finally asked a question that he wanted to have asked. His expression returned to the inscrutable look he had maintained through most of the interview. 'I can't stop you,' he said, and I left.

"You know, Rocky, after I had been a journalist for a few years, I told my father that in one sense he finally got the athlete that he was hoping to have as his offspring. I'd learned that one has to become a verbal fencer to do good interviews, especially when your sources don't really want you to know anything. My meeting with Adam Baxter, the principal of Chestnut Ridge High School, the then newly reigning state high school football champion, taxed my fencing skills to the utmost.

"I understand the public's distress with the many members of the press who shred people's privacy about matters that only the worst kind of hypocrite would assert must be revealed because of the people's right to know. On the other hand, I am equally annoyed by people who refuse to be candid about subjects that are legitimate matters of public interest, especially when public feelings are misdirected through the persistence of false impressions. A reporter is justified in doing some fencing to get the true story in such instances.

"However, principal Baxter proved to be a fencer of superior skill to my own. To begin with, he questioned that I was telling the truth about the existence of the anonymous letter. His smirk when I had to admit that I hadn't brought it with me was annoying. I stated my willingness to return with the letter if he would assure me that I would receive a direct answer that the allegation in the letter was true or false. He would make no such commitment out of respect for Coach Robb's privacy, he asserted. I asked if he did not recognize, in view of the popularity of the high school football team with the community at large, that Coach Robb's sudden resignation without explanation on the heels of the team's greatest success in the school's history was the topic of endless discussion in the community. Baxter said that that was understandable, but after all, Coach Robb had the right to live his life as he chose.

"It was fortunate that the fencing was merely metaphoric. I'd loved to have jabbed him literally at that point. His sole question was to ask if I'd talked to Coach Robb. When I told him that Robb had declined to comment, his face showed an expression of relief and satisfaction. He launched into effusive praise of Tank as a coach and a man. It seemed that Tank's silence made him just as praiseworthy than his coaching success.

"I said, 'Mr. Baxter, aside from your responsibilities as the principal, don't you personally find Coach Robb's decision to stop coaching at the very height of his success puzzling?' Mr. Baxter looked positively Buddha-like in responding that he was sure that Coach Robb had his reasons, that they must be personal and that they should be respected. 'His privacy should not be intruded on,' Baxter said, looking positively saintly. I wanted to say that I had never seen anyone who would have been more happy to have his privacy intruded on than Tank Robb, but the statement did not seem like a wise strategy.

"My report to the editor of my lack of success in getting any background story on Robb's resignation got me the standard lecture on the need to do some digging to get a good story. To stop the near inevitable illustration of how they did it in his day, I suggested a change of approach to exploring the anonymous letter. I suggested that we do a human interest story on Robb himself. While Robb was not an engaging personality, even to the football fanatical townies, he did enjoy the popularity that a winning coach had in a community and region besotted with intense interest in high school football. As a starting point for pursuing the story, I suggested, I could talk to the high school assistant principal Dave Christiansen, who had been a teammate of Robb's in college. Using Christiansen's viewpoint on the rise of his old teammate to the pinnacle of success as the coach of the current state champion as an opener, I could detail Robb's entire coaching career and conclude with the mysterious, unexplained retirement from coaching at an early age.

"My editor agreed on the biographical story, stipulating that I was to keep my ears open for any information relating to the anonymous allegation that might leak out from my interviews. I slightly knew Mr. Christiansen. I always thought of him as a 'Mr.' and used the title even though he had invited me to call him by his first name when my dad had introduced us. We had met casually a couple of times, but I had never interviewed him for a story until I set out to do the piece on Tank Robb. The interview was just as you'd have expected because you know what he was like, all warm toward his listener and effusively positive about anyone who was being discussed. It would have been nauseating if it hadn't been so obviously sincere. So I got the unstinting story of Tank the great running back, Tank the dedicated student of the game, Tank the stern taskmaster with the big-hearted concern for his players. I had to restrain myself from saying that I was writing a newspaper article, not proposing him for sainthood. Don't misunderstand my reaction. Robb had been a very good coach, but Dave Christiansen could make the school janitor sound like a vital force in the educational process by sticking to the truthful positives."

Rocky nodded. "He always looked for the best in everyone and always appreciated a person's efforts and contributions. It's one of the reasons his college friends liked him and stayed in touch with him over the years."

"When I had more of Robb-the-Paragon stuff than I would ever need, I gave up the interview and just began to chat with him. I knew that he had been a fine athlete himself, so I asked if he had ever had the urge to coach football himself. He shook his head and said that his career had gone in exactly the direction that he wanted. He liked doing school administration, he said, because he thought he was helping the education of more kids in that role than if he were still in the classroom. I confessed that I didn't know exactly what his duties were. He mentioned duties about some important things like curriculum development and supervision and also securing teaching materials and instructional equipment. Then he listed a staggering number of bureaucratic details, which included among them one that struck me as possibly having some relevance to the mystery of the reason for Tank Robb's untimely resignation.

"Dave Christiansen said that his office processed the grade reports for the entire high school. It was the place to which all the teachers sent their grades and where the reports were prepared that went to the parents of each student. I said that it didn't sound like much fun to be the one that has to pass on the bad news. He said that there was a positive side. It was his job to identify the students who were in serious grade trouble so that they could be referred to the school's counselors. Timely intervention, he said, saved many students from becoming dropouts. That, he assured me, was one of his greatest satisfactions. Using my best reporter's effort to sound and look casual, which means as close to seeming uninterested as one can muster, I asked how often he performed the task of examining grade reports? He answered that it was not as often as he would like for the early identification of students who ought to be in counseling or tutoring. He specified that he did so at the middle and end of each semester. In fact, he said, he had recently finished the task for the middle of the fall semester.

"You see the relevance of what he said. If Dave Christiansen personally examined the grade reports for all the students in the high school, he would know if some athlete had become ineligible to participate due to a failing grade or grades. One could infer that no member of the newly crowned state champions had become ineligible during the season or before the championship game, or it would have been a topic of wide and anguished discussion. Of course, if Tank Robb had played an ineligible player that could have been a reason that he had been forced to resign. Such an violation was not apparent, since the high school had not announced that it was forfeiting the state championship. That could mean either than there had been no impropriety or that Tank Robb had been considered more expendable than the championship. In view of local community values, you and I both know that is not an outrageous possibility.

"At that point in my meeting with Mr. Christiansen, I told him about the contents of the anonymous letter which had reached my editor's office. I asked if he thought that there was any truth in it. He frowned and examined the floor of his office thoughtfully for a long time.

"Finally he nodded his head and looked at me. 'It is possible that even good people do some very foolish things at times,' he said.

"Do you think that the board forced Coach Robb's resignation," I asked. 'I wouldn't have official knowledge of anything like that,' he said.

"For a guy who normally didn't fence, it was a pretty good parry.

"How about unofficial knowledge?" I tried. 'It puzzles me why someone would write such a thing,' he said, shaking his head once again.

"Could you speculate? I asked for a final try. 'Speculation is never a wise activity for a school administrator,' Mr. Christiansen smiled at me.

"Obviously I wasn't going to get any further exploring my own speculation. I returned his smile and thanked him for his input and went off to consider if there might be some truth to the anonymous letter. If it was true that Tank Robb had been forced to resign, I could think of no other likely reason for it than some regulatory impropriety. The amount of discretionary money floating around high school football are not large enough to be a temptation to anyone except the desperate or the small minded. Robb didn't fit either of those profiles.

"The are an unfortunate number of ways to cheat in high school athletics; however, the most likely way is to use players who are not eligible to participate. Obviously, that ineligible player or players would most likely be people of exceptional talent to make the risk tempting enough to succumb to. In fact, Tank Robb's Chestnut Ridge High Bruins had two such exceptional players in the recently completed season. One was the quarterback, who is an extraordinary passer. However, he is an unlikely possibility to have had grade difficulties. As word has it that, even though a junior, he was being heavily recruited by several ivy leagues universities not noted for lowering their admission standards to stock their athletic teams. The other exceptional player of the team was a running back of unusual speed and considerable size. Though he is certainly not a scholar, there has been no hint of his being in grade difficulty during the season.

"I was tempted to meet with Mr. Christiansen again and ask him if the halfback, Claude Pruitt, who graduated this spring, had had grade difficulties in the past fall. I decided against doing that for a very pragmatic reason. If an ineligibility for poor grades had occurred, Dave Christiansen had been complicit in the wrongdoing, as much as it pained me to recognize the fact regarding the man my father had admired above all others for his integrity.

"I considered by what other avenue than going to Christiansen I could explore the possibility of Claude Pruitt's ineligibility. Since the possibility was not even worthy of being called a good hunch, I could not do so openly. I couldn't ask for the boy's schedule listing who his teachers were, not only because it would be a breech of privacy, but because the very query would produce an alarm that would close off most possibilities of getting information.

"A little common sense deduction was called for. What classes would a not particularly academically inclined jock take? Some subjects, like English, history and a smattering of science and mathematics, would be required, of course. Pruitt being a senior, he was probably past the point of having to take the latter two subjects. Even history was unlikely to be required all four years of high school. Taking English every year was absolutely inescapable if you were figuring on an athletic scholarship to get into college. An interview with the boy's English teacher, purportedly to do a feature on the star running back of the state champions, would be a plausible starting point. The matter of his grades could come up only as part of a comprehensive picture.

"My first problem was that Chestnut Ridge High School was large enough that there would be several possibilities of who had been Claude Pruitt's English teacher. I puzzled over this difficulty a while before a solution that should have been obvious occurred to me. There was an English teacher at Chestnut Ridge, Portia Littleton, whose husband had been a teammate of Tank Robb in college. I could interview her for my possible feature story on Robb and tangentially find out if she was Pruitt's teacher or if she knew who was. I see that puzzled look on your face, Rocky. You don't recollect anyone named Littleton who played with you and Tank Robb in college. Portia Littleton is a widow; you probably remember her by her married name, Castor. She was Rich Castor's wife, and, when he died, she went back to her maiden name. There's a story behind than that I only know thanks to my mother, who is emphatic that giving up that name was the most sensitive and sanity-saving thing that Portia Littleton did after her husband died.

"Are you interested in the story? That's not a very decisive nod, but I'll take it as a yes. Perhaps you recall Castor dating what my mother described as a very good-looking and slender co-ed with brown hair and a great smile?"

"I'm remembering now. I didn't know they'd married. Rich was unusually handsome himself. They made a magazine-ad type perfect couple, as I recall."

"So I was told, Unfortunately, that situation did not continue years later. My parents used to socialize with the Castors. Later, the friendship dissolved because my parents could not endure the cruel things that Rich Castor would say to Portia in their presence."

Rocky nodded, "I was never crazy about Rich. Pretty but masculine sometimes comes with too much ego, in my experience. What was his beef with Portia? Not good in bed? Too good in bed? Too good a housekeeper? Or not good enough? Spoiled the meals? Or spoiled the kids?"

"In fact, they had two quite nice kids who became happy and successful adults who are still in frequent contact with their mother. Unfortunately, like many people, Portia began to gain weight when she was still rather young. Before long, she reached the pretty-but-plump level, as my mom calls it. She never managed to take the weight off. Rich, who somehow never seemed to gain a pound all of his rather short life, nagged Portia about her weight publicly. The terms he used for her were as cruel as you could possibly imagine, according to my mother. My mom said she could have crowned Rich with something the way he constantly belittled Portia. But Portia just bowed her head and looked chastened.

"Intermittently Portia went on another diet, according to my mom, but to no avail."

"That's hell of a way to live for anyone, but even more so for a woman who'd been so beautiful in her youth and was married to a good-looking idiot."

"Rich never seemed to age and stayed trim all his life. My mother used to hope that he'd run face first into a tree branch or something and pick up some scars. You probably know that he died in his early forties of a heart attack. Not long after, his wife went back to her maiden name and started teaching at Old Fort High."

Rocky shrugged, "I guess that her marriage was so distasteful that she didn't even want to carry her husband's name any more?"

"No need to guess, I assure you. She made it plain enough to my parents."

Rocky frowned, "So she hasn't retired yet?"

"No, fortunately for me. As I said, I went to see her because she was most likely to be Claude Pruitt's English teacher or know who was. She was, unlike her former self as the wife of Rich Castor, a woman of sunny disposition. She kept me answering questions about my mother, my wife and children and every other common acquaintance she suspected we might share.

"It was a pretty long time before I had a chance to tell her my purported purpose for being there. I said that I was doing a feature piece on Tank Robb and wondered if she could give me some impressions of her college contemporary and current colleague.

"She sighed and said, 'Oh, dear, Brad, I'm afraid that I can't be any help to you.' Even her apologetic expression had its own pleasantness. 'I never was a football fan, you see. Even though my ex-husband--I mean *deceased* husband, don't I--played in college, I never could get interested. I've known Tank, of course, but we've never had more than a brief conversation in the faculty lunchroom from time to time, so I can't really tell you much about him.'

"Did he ever talk to you about any of his players? It would be relevant to know if he cared about how they were doing academically. You know, if he cared about them beyond their participation on the team." Ms. Littleton nodded affirmatively. 'Yes, there were a few occasions when he did ask me about one of his boys. But you know, I don't get many athletes in my class. Perhaps you know that the school offers three levels of English courses. One course is for high-ability, college bound students. The brighter athletes would be in that one. There's another course for students whose education will most likely end with high school, either by their choice or from their academic limitations. As you might imagine, quite a few athletes are in that version of the English program. The third version of the English program, the one I teach, is for students of above-average but not extraordinary ability. Quite a few of these students are college bound, of course. It is a demanding curriculum, not the sort of thing that a young man focused on his athletic skills would normally select, but I do get a few.'

"I suggested that to me, her course sounded like exactly the choice that an athlete would make if he were hoping for a scholarship and weren't capable enough or motivated enough for the advanced curriculum.

"Ms. Littleton said, 'I suppose that's true.' I asked if she had had any of Coach Robb's football players in class this past fall. 'Now that I think of it, there was one,' she said, her eyes lighting up at the realization. 'Silly of me not to think of him right away, him being the star runner and all.'

"I suppose Coach Robb would be concerned whether he was doing all right," I said, trying as best I could to sound off-hand.

"Portia Littleton smiled. 'No cause for the coach to be concerned about Claude Pruitt. He is a perfectly adequate student. I've no doubt that when he is able to make up the mid-term test he missed, I'll be recording a B grade for him as usual.'

"Sounds like the boy's run into some bad luck," I said. Ms. Littleton sighed sympathetically. 'Yes, his father's illness has caused him to miss quite a bit of school in the last couple months or so. He'll soon make up the incomplete, I'm sure.'

"I said, "That's good to know. I suppose the assistant principal was as concerned as the coach when he saw the grade report."

"Ms. Littleton blushed before she responded. 'Yes, he did speak to me about the grade report. It was so embarrassing.'

"I asked her if Mr. Christiansen had been upset about Pruitt's incomplete. 'No,' she said with a shake of her head. 'He never mentioned it. He was concerned that my grade sheet hadn't reached his office on the Friday when it was due. I was so sure that I'd taken it to his mail box on Friday, but when he came to ask about it on Monday, there it was on my desk under a stack of mail I hadn't opened yet. I was so embarrassed. I don't know what happens to me sometimes. I plan doing something and, having imagined doing it, I manage to convince myself that I've actually done it. Dave and I joked about it. He says he does the same thing sometimes. He said that we both must be getting old.'

"She smiled in recollection. 'Dave suggested that I'd better not mention having missed the submission deadline, or they'd be putting us both out to pasture. I sure that your father often mentioned how nice Dave Christiansen was. A kinder, sweeter man never lived.'

"After agreeing with her statement about Mr. Christiansen, I asked Portia Littleton if she had anything further about Coach Robb that she wanted to say. After she nodded negatively, she said earnestly and at length how nice it was to see me and that I must give my mother her regards. I left wondering how Rich Castor could ever have been unkind to such a likable woman.

"The interview with Ms. Littleton gave me, for the first time, something to speculate about with regard to Tank Robb's mysterious resignation. Of course, it could be that she had absentmindedly forgotten to turn in the grade report that would have made Robb's star running back ineligible to play in the state championship football game the next day. However, that struck me as doubtful. Equally doubtful was the possibility that Ms. Littleton knew the consequences of the incomplete she had recorded for Claude Pruitt. I can't believe that she deliberately withheld the grade report to let the boy play because she was unwilling to deny him perhaps the most important activity of his young life.

"If that were the case, her lack of interest in athletics was an adroit deception. I thought of the round. rosy-cheeked face and smiley eyes that were a classic portrait of pleasantry and openness and concluded that deliberate deception on her part was unlikely. The one other possibility was that someone had returned to her desk the grade report that she had taken to Christiansen in time for the deadline. Perhaps there were a number of people who would have done that in view of the fanaticism about the high school team that was universal in town that season.

"But a person motivated by concern for the outcome of the game would have had to know the eligibility rules well enough to realize that an incomplete would put Pruitt in grade difficulty as much as a low grade would. That narrowed the possibilities considerably. In my mind, that lowered the possibilities to two: Dave Christiansen and Tank Robb. The motivation for Robb to have returned the report to Ms. Littleton's desk before the game, the favorable outcome of which was the high point of his coaching career, was obvious.

"Why Dave Christiansen, by public reputation a paragon of integrity, would have done so was more complicated to speculate. He was a former jock. Maybe the high school's winning was important enough to him that he would bend the rules in an instance within his confidential control. But then why would he subsequently blow the whistle and force Tank Robb's resignation? It was possible that there was animosity between them simmering from years ago in college when they were teammates. However, Christiansen seemed like a poor candidate to have nursed an injury for years to score a really satisfying revenge.

"On the other hand, he and Tank could have been such good buddies that he buried the grades so as not to spoil his buddy's chances for a state championship. Eventually, I concluded that all the scenarios that I imagined were legitimate possibilities of greater or lesser probability. In such circumstances, there is only one thing for an aggressive reporter to do. Confront the likely wrongdoers with the damaging speculations and hope for a guilty admission or a revealing denial that provided an avenue for further pursuit of the matter.

"I doubted that Tank Robb was much of a candidate for my pulling off a revealing confrontation. I have to confess that his potential for at least some very extreme verbal unpleasantness and at worst physical violence also deterred me from wanting to confront Tank. Like many another reporters, when having to choose between talking to an uncivilized and a civilized source, I opted for the more potentially pliable. That is not an admirable tendency in a reporter, I admit, but I chose it. I resolved to ask to meet again with Dave Christiansen.

"The next day, when I entered Mr. Christiansen's office, I reminded myself to be cautious in my tactics. I respected him too much to engage in circuitous sparring in the hopes of producing some unguarded statement that would confirm my suspicions. Looking into that strong and open face that seemed incapable of guile, I adopted an expression that I hoped would match the candor I intended.

"I began, 'I have developed a theory about Coach Robb's resignation based on the assertions in the anonymous letter that I spoke to you about before. I wonder if you'd confirm it for me if you can?'

"He smiled at me with that broad and easy smile which is part of the mental image of him that everyone who knew him carries. 'How many years has it been that I've asked you to call me Dave?'

"I answered, 'I've always been pleased that you've invited me to do that, but somehow it would just seem disrespectful.'

"He laughed and said, 'So you don't call anyone my age by their first name?'

"He continued to grin as he waited for the obvious answer. 'No, it's a matter of relating to certain people,' I explained.

"'Then you don't feel friendly enough to me that you can use my first name?' The playful spirit in which he asked the question prompted a similar tone to my response, though I felt like I was losing control of the interview. I asked, 'You wouldn't be evading answering my question, would you?'

"He chuckled and looked as close to having a guilty expression as I'd ever seen him have. 'Maybe I am, but,' he said, quickly turning serious, 'you know that I said that I wouldn't comment on the anonymous letter.'

"I nodded agreement. 'Right, I don't expect you to. I just want to tell you my theory about the reason that Coach Robb's resignation may have been coerced and have you react to it. Would you do that?'

He studied the top of his desk thoughtfully for a long time before he nodded that he would.

"'I think that Coach Robb's star running back Claude Pruitt was ineligible to play in the championship game. Robb knew it and played him anyway. The ineligibility wasn't discovered until after the game because Robb had removed the grade report that Pruitt's English teacher had submitted to your office and put it back on her desk to create the impression it had never been submitted. When you retrieved the grade report on the Monday after the game, you reported the violation of eligibility to senior administration. They and the school board must have decided not to report the violation and forfeit the championship, but they also decided to salve their consciences by insisting that Robb resign to avoid embarrassment to him and the school.'

"Christiansen looked at me silently a long time. His brow was furrowed and his lips were clenched as though he was struggling to prevent the escape of any sound. He looked at me eye-to-eye, sadness emerging in his expression. 'That's quite a theory,' he murmured and rubbed his chin pensively.

"Is it what happened?" I pressed.

"Finally, he sighed and said, 'Brad, unless you can get a number of people: Tank, me, the principal, the superintendent, a school board composed of some of the most respected citizens in town, to admit to some unsavory behavior, you'll never have anything but your speculation.'

"The way I see it, you didn't do anything inappropriate. In fact, you're the only one who looks good if I've got the story accurately.'

"His face lit with a grin. 'You think its better to be seen as a self-serving prig than a co-conspirator in a plot to save the town a major embarrassment?'

"'Your action wasn't self-serving; it was strictly principled,' I responded. I felt certain that there was no reason for him to feel jeopardized by admitting the truth. His confirmation of my scenario alone would be sufficient verification to permit me write the story as fact. Christiansen shook his head, 'If you think that a town full of people bursting with pride in their state champions will see your perception of an action which, I take pains to emphasize, I don't confirm having happened, you know remarkably little about human nature for a journalist.'

"Continuing to pursue my theory as a fact, I tried working on his conscience. 'You can't condone what Robb did to Portia Littleton. He tried to shift the responsibility entirely to her shoulders. The town would condemn her mercilessly.'

"Christiansen looked at me with an abundance of skepticism. 'You think that a town full of football fanatics wouldn't prefer to see her as careless and addlebrained rather than the victim of a trick by an ambitious football coach?'

"His gaze became piercing. 'You want Portia Littleton to say publicly that she is now sure she brought her grades to my office even though she'd earlier been convinced that she hadn't done so? You'd be comfortable to let one of the most caring and capable teachers in this high school look forgetful at best and senile at worst?'

"You really think that the town wants to keep the championship even if it wasn't won by the rules?" I asked.

"Dave Christiansen sighed resignedly. 'I don't really have to answer that, do I? In fact, I don't want to answer any other questions either. I'm sorry, Brad, but I really don't want to continue this interview.' He rose to his feet.

"I had the feeling that if I didn't accept that the interview was over, that this most civilized of men would do something uncharacteristically forceful. As I rose to go, I did something uncharacteristic myself, at least I hope it is. I said, 'I could write my story from a speculative approach, you know. I could just say that the rumors are simply that and let readers leap to their own conclusions. It's common enough for reporters to do that.'

"Dave Christiansen looked at me squarely, with a tinge of sorrow in his face. 'That is unfortunately the case with some reporters. If you do that, Brad. I have greatly misjudged you.'

"I've carried the way he looked at me in my mind to this day. I guess that is why I never wrote the story. But I have no doubt that I figured out the reason for Tank Robb's mysterious resignation at the height of his coaching career."

Ending his long silence as the reporter had told his story, Rocky nodded agreement at the journalist son of his college friend. "Still, one could give credence to Tank's assertion that Dave did what he did to improve his chances to move up the administrative ladder."

Brad Wright shook his head in rejection of the idea. "The high school principal was past retirement age already when the championship season happened. And Dave Christiansen didn't need to do anything manipulative to polish his image. Everyone from the faculty through the student body already saw him as the next principal. All the board had to do was confirm the obvious."

Rocky smiled. "So Tank ended up working on the teaching staff of the man he believes wrecked his coaching career. Nice."

"You know, I'm not convinced that Robb really believes that," Brad Wright said. "My guess is that he denigrates Dave Christiansen because he realizes that Dave Christiansen saved his teaching career, and he can't stand being beholden."

"You think so?"

The journalist spread his hands as though to emphasize the plausibility of his statement. "Does it seem like the Dave Christiansen that all his friends admired for his integrity to have gone along with the cover up that let the town relish its football glory when it was deceptively won?"

"Not really, I admit," nodded Rocky.

Wright's expression was almost mischievous, perhaps from being a reporter who was relishing possession of a delicious secret. "Is it too farfetched to imagine Dave Christiansen insisting on a teaching job for his old teammate as the price of his silence about the cover up of the tainted championship?"

Rocky nodded affirmatively. "I could see Dave stretching his principles far enough to see that a friend continued to have a career rather than suffering public embarrassment and possibly being unemployable in his chosen profession. Dave would think that Tank's loss of the work he loved best was punishment enough under the circumstances."

The journalist nodded his agreement. "And Christiansen's reward was lifelong vilification by the man who benefited from a rare compromise of his principles."

Rocky chuckled heartily. "Dave became a school administrator. No one else knows better than they that no good deed goes unpunished."

"I thought reporters knew that better than anyone else," Wright said wryly.

"I'm not surprised that you have some experience with the phenomenon," Rocky consoled. "But isn't it at least a rarer occurrence for a sports journalist than political or news reporters??"

"Not less frequent, but perhaps not as searing an experience in reporting other local news."

"Have you done some work in that area?" Rocky asked.

"A long and boring story," Wright sighed dismissively.

"Actually, I have the time if you've got the inclination to tell it," said Rocky.

The journalist shuffled papers on his desk for a good while before he began somewhat reluctantly. "About a dozen years ago I asked if I could move out of sports and do general reporting. Since the publisher and editor had always liked my stuff well enough and since there are always plenty of young guys coming out of college who are dying to write sports, they agreed to give me a try. Soon, I was covering everything from bake sales through local and state politics. Everything seemed to go very well. There was good feedback from both readers and the people and groups that I covered. Management seemed well satisfied with my handling of what they deemed more important work.

"I suppose that's why they decided to expand my duties when a cost-cutting opportunity came up. One of the assistant editors who did layout, which is not a fancy computerized activity on a small local daily, even to this day, left. My duties were expanded to laying out some pages of news copy and the ads that appeared there."

Rocky held up a hand palm outward in a gesture of restraint. "Let me guess. The editorial work diminished the caliber of your reporting and some embarrassing error crept into one of your stories, probably a political piece."

"No," Brad sighed reflectively, "there wasn't a factual problem with anything I wrote, but I stepped on a political mine nevertheless."

Rocky risked an amiable smile. "You're even more creative than I imagined."

"This required no creativity, I assure you," Brad said. He lapsed into an inert silence.

"So, what happened?" Rocky asked with evident curiosity.

Wright looked torn between wanting to unburden himself and fearful of re-treading ground that was no less painful for being familiar and long past. "I told you it's a long story."

"I'd love to hear it."

Wright betrayed a wistful grin. "Politics around here is usually a fairly somnambulant activity. The Republicans have held a two to one or better voter registration margin around here since the Lincoln administration. So, it's not surprising that for one hundred and forty years, the district has sent a Republican to the state legislature. Even in the depths of the depression this legislative district did not succumb to the evil blandishments of the Democrats under Franklin Roosevelt."

"That's what I'd call staunch," Rocky chuckled.

"I'll illustrate how staunch," Brad grinned, warming to his subject. "I remember the first time I mentioned FDR to the barber who used to cut my hair back then. He pointed with his scissors to a little, ancient-looking radio on a table against he wall. 'You see that radio?' he said. 'That radio has never had Roosevelt's voice on it. Every time that sonofabitch was going to talk, I turned it off.'

"Now, that old boy was not up for any 'We have nothing to fear but fear itself,'" Brad grinned. "You'd never believe what a pleasant, rational man he was on any other subject than any subject associated with the Democrats. He was typical of the majority of voters around here. He predicted the collapse of social security till the day he died."

"God, he may turn out to be right," Rocky said.

"Maybe not," Brad smiled wanly. "Journalists on rare occasion observe an outbreak of rational self-interest on the part of the public at large. The impending collapse of social security may produce one of those times."

"I suppose the demise of the program would produce a chorus of 'I told you so's' around here," Rocky speculated.

"Not to the extent it would have at the time I'm talking about," said Brad. "The region is politically schizophrenic now. The little episode I was involved in was the beginning of that development."

Rocky settled back in his chair, signaling his desire to have the journalist son of his college friend continue his story, "The year after I began working in news and grunt editorial work was an non-presidential election year—just congressional, state legislative and local offices up for election. That's generally a situation responded to with rampant voter apathy here as just about everywhere else. But that year turned out to be very different. The Wednesday Morning Businessmen's Bible Study Group, an organization until that time unknown to the general public, decided that their commitment to the Lord's work prompted that they should become politically active.

"Everyone's biases, including mine, naturally attribute differing reasons for their decision," Brad continued. "Cynics say that they realized that the group could be an avenue for personal political power, a means to accomplish the selfish desires of some of their number for elected office. It's likely that the entrenched Republican Party handlers either didn't know much about these recently repentant sinners. That is, by the way, not an unfair description. The group had its share of adulterers, boozers and fast-buck artists, so it wasn't surprising that the party regulars were leery of them. Many rank and file Republicans insisted that it was only fair to treat them as sincere. These party loyalists sincerely believe that government should be based on religious tenets--their religion, of course. Hence they were pleased at the political activism of the Bible Study Group.

"In the case of the local legislative seat, the Republican regulars were totally unconcerned about the primary soon to occur. The incumbent was a common sense centrist whose willingness to work for his constituents regardless of party affiliation had reduced Democratic opposition to mere tokenism for fourteen years. Even when a member of the Bible Study Group filed to run in the Republican primary, the incumbent and the party organization was not moved to action.

"What is far from an unusual event in American politics occurred. The Biblical businessmen worked zealously for their man. They went to the churches and urged them to support a Christian man inspired by the Lord and newly washed in the blood of the lamb. They argued that their candidate would bring desperately needed Christian values into the legislature. The morning after the primary the incumbent and a large number of Republicans who hadn't voted were surprised to find themselves about to lose a highly acceptable legislator whose fourteen years of seniority had given the district a substantial clout in state level decision-making. In addition, the Democrats, who had nominated another unelectable nonentity because the centrist Republican had served them well, were equally surprised.

"The most upset among those who had been satisfied with the incumbent legislator were the faculty of the state university. You, having played against The Seneca State Braves for your and my dad's alma mater, remember that Seneca State is on the edge of town here."

Rocky pointed a cautioning finger at the story teller. "We didn't just play them when I was in school. We kicked their ass four years in a row, which was admittedly a rare feat at Glassport State."

"I recollect my father mentioning that a couple of million times every year when the annual Seneca-Glassport game was approaching."

"I didn't mean to interrupt," Rocky apologized with feigned gravity. "I just wanted to be sure the record was clear."

"Duly noted," Wright said. "As I said, the faculty of Seneca State was greatly alarmed at losing the incumbent Republican legislator even though the prevailing party registration among them was almost three to one Democratic. It was quite understandable. The incumbent Republican was an alumnus. He always looked out for the old school. Not only because he felt sentimental about the place, but because it is the biggest payroll in town and vital to the local economy. It's no surprise that the committee assignment he most cherished was the chairmanship of the higher education committee, where he supported everything from buildings to salaries for the local university. Besides, keeping the professors happy prevented the development of any real opposition in the general election. He could always count on the Democrats nominating a sacrificial lamb who conducted an under-funded, pro forma campaign to build visibility for seeking some other elective job later.

"When these academic Democrats realized what they would be losing if the chairman of the higher education committee of the legislature would no longer be the special friend of the university, they decided to mount a write in campaign on his behalf. He didn't immediately accept their offer. Obviously he was warned by the Republican organization that his political career was finished if he ran against the party endorsed candidate.

"The overwhelming Republican registration advantage being what it was, the chances of the success of a write in campaign, at best a long shot, were practically nil. He'd be bucking not only his former party's endorsed and well-funded candidate but a Democratic opponent as well. Besides, the Democrats would no doubt be energized by the possibility of taking advantage of a split in Republican votes that could give them a success after one hundred and forty years of futility. The presence two competitors in the Republican primary had encouraged them to nominate someone more formidable than the usual quasi high school student government president that they normally ran.

"Actually, if the Republican party war horses hadn't threatened the incumbent so heavy-handedly, he might not have run in the general election and bided his time until the next primary. But the threats of the old dragon lady who was the party county chairman eventually backfired. The assurances of the university faculty about the campaign they would run for him and the money they would contribute to it made him decide to run as an independent.

"As you might expect, it was the most exciting and contentious campaign around here in anyone's memory. With no presidential or gubernatorial campaign to compete with it for attention, it garnered every bit of local attention that could be spared from the county fair, high school sports and network television talk shows. The staunch Republicans made the write in campaign sound like the greatest betrayal of genuine American politics short of armed rebellion. The Democratic loyalists were stimulated by the possibility of ending one hundred and forty years of electoral futility and the university faculty activists were viewed either extremely favorably or negatively depending on one's party loyalty."

Rocky could not restrain his amusement. "Sounds like it had everything a journalist would want in a political campaign except a sex scandal."

"What makes you think that the real or imagined morals of the academics backing the write in candidate didn't come in for considerable comment? The religious fundamentalists in town have never been comfortable with that nest of Godless communists and sexual profligates on the edge of town. The supporters of the apostate who would not accept the decision of the 20% of the voters who turned out for the primary was challenging the fine Christian candidate who had won fair and square. That view got considerable attention in Republican campaign meetings and campaign literature."

"It must have been a fun campaign to report," Rocky said.

"At first it was, but the build up of intensity caused me continual annoyance. I couldn't write a sentence to anyone's satisfaction. Every reader seemed to think I'd made his candidate look undeservedly bad and the other two guys look unwarrantedly good. Depending on which candidate a reader was committed to, the same paragraph was either insufficiently laudatory or poisonously unfair.

"At least two months before the election, everyone's mind had been made up, if it hadn't been made up the morning after the primary, which was probably the case for two-thirds of the voters. So the last two months were devoted to stating and re-stating every promise, allegation, and rebuttal that had long since been asserted. We never before had so much money spent on political ads, or have had since, if one takes inflation into account."

"Your publisher must have been delighted at the bonanza."

"Oh, he was," Brad snorted, "once he made clear that I was to handle the political ads fairly."

"Why, Bradley." Rocky gasped in mock horror, "you were being unfair. I'm shocked."

"I'll confess to you the unfairness I was accused of, Mr. Rocco," Brad Wright said with the same feigned seriousness with which Rocky's accusation had been made, "and you can tell me where I went wrong."

Brad's face showed an unpleasant recollection and began, "One day just before lunch, I was finishing pasting up the national and world roundup sections of the news, as we called them, not a difficult task, really; just a matter of deciding how much of the wire service copy could be fitted in around the all important local ads that were the paper's bread and butter. Then there appeared before me the man who brought in the political ads for the Republican candidate for the legislature. His appearance, just as that of the ad writer for the write-in candidate, had become a daily event. The unusually full campaign coffers of these two opponents were applied to a daily attempt to keep the support of party loyalists or woo the imagined number of uncommitted voters in the district.

"The editor-in-chief and the publisher were delighted with the extra revenue and only regretted that the Democratic candidate didn't have equal resources. I was less pleased with one aspect of the contest. Both candidates' operatives challenged deadlines so closely and pleaded for the most desirable location for their latest salvos after the task of fitting everything in was near completion. My attempts to anticipate their space requirements were usually thrown off by the latest infusion of campaign contributions or intermittent fears that their current resources would not last until the election two months hence.

"The Republican ad man was generally a bit harder to work with because of his righteous attitude. His physical appearance was ill-suited to the role of meek messenger of God-centered politics. Rumor had it that his flattened nose had been acquired when both he and another disputant declined to turn the other cheek over a real estate deal. This behavior, of course, had occurred before he had found God. Perhaps I lack respect for repentance, but I find it much more tolerable when it is not combined with evangelism and self-aggrandizing public religiosity.

"I tried to avoid letting my concern with my approaching deadline color my greeting. 'Good morning, Mr. Carver, you have some advertising copy for today's paper?' I asked.

He peered at me with considerable gravity and answered. "It's not ready yet, but it shouldn't take me long if you'll just cooperate."

"I'd be happy to. What can I do for you?" I offered, expecting a question about type style, text arrangement or some such matter.

"If the write-in candidate's placing any advertising today, I'd like to see it."

"I suppressed my surprise and looked carefully to see if he was departing from his usual grave demeanor and was joking with me. He betrayed no sign of humor. However, he had never indulged in amiability before, so I thought I just might not be clued to his style of humor. When he repeated his request with emphasis, I concluded that he was quite serious.

"I said that I didn't think that that would be appropriate. He said, 'Why not? Shouldn't we have the chance to respond to any positions that they publish? That's only fair, isn't it?'

"Yes, sir, of course you have a right to respond if there is anything to respond to. There's plenty of time and opportunity for you to do that after their piece appears." Mr. Carver looked unable to decide whether I was obstreperous or stupid.

" 'But I want to do it now. Its not right to let a lie or false impression stand uncorrected for a day or any amount of time. The voters deserve to know the truth before they are misled. Its much harder to correct these false impressions later.' "

"I'm sure that your opponents would say the same thing. But for today you are asking to take an advantage that is not open to them. If they could, I'm sure they'd want to rebut your rebuttal and you'd want to rebut that. There's no fair way but to have you both see the other's argument in print."

"He said, 'Political campaigns are for the purpose of getting differing view before the voters, aren't they? I want to get ours out at the same time as theirs.'

"I said, 'However, I don't think that my responsibilities as a newspaper man will permit me to let you examine your opposition's positions before they are published.'

"He said, 'Your responsibility as a newspaper man is to be fair, and fairness requires that you let me prevent anything unfair to my candidate being put before the public before our making a response.'

"It was clear to me by this time that Mr. Carver thought either that I was too dense to understand the obvious logic of what he was saying or that I favored his opposition. 'I'm sorry, Mr. Carver, I just don't think that I should do it. The fairest thing is that all candidates be in the same position to be surprised and deal with it when it happens.' I gave the statement as much finality as I could convey without being rude.

"He shook his head in disbelief more than annoyance, I thought, and parted with a curt, 'We'll see about this.'

"And did you see about it?" Rocky asked.

"Oh, yes," Brad said with a pursing of his lips that suggested another unpleasant memory. "Either Mr. Carver was invested with the prescience to anticipate on that day and most others for the remaining two months of the campaign the arguments that the write in candidate's staff was featuring in their ads that day or my superiors here were letting Carver see the opposition copy before we went to press."

Rocky smiled wryly, "Did you suggest to your editor that you would like to do a story on the remarkable mental powers of someone in the Republican campaign?"

"I didn't see much of a point. I know the political allegiance of the publisher of this paper. I was not surprised that his concept of fairness was the same as Carver's. As to the editor-in-chief's political leanings they are whatever the publisher says they should be. I have to chuckle every time I read one of those right wing rants about a liberal bias in the press. I knew then that it was true, and may still be, that the majority of reporters tend to be left of center in their personal views. However, I firmly believe that if they get too far left of center in what they write, you can bet they will be pursuing other employment opportunities in very short order."

Rocky nodded mirthlessly. "I've always thought that it took a uniquely American frame of mind to believe that people who own newspapers or television networks would let their publications overtly favor political views far different than their own. I respect your sense of realism. There was nothing you could do without foolish personal sacrifice."

"I did do something, ineffectual though it was, " Wright said. "The remarkable powers of the Republican campaign organization did not escape the notice of the man who did the write in candidate's print ads."

Rocky feigned astonishment. "Don't tell me he was a professor yet still someone able to add two and two and get four?"

"Remarkable, isn't it?" Wright answered with mock seriousness. "He stated his conclusion to me with some vigor. Although he was a bright man with some sense of humor, he was prone to irritability. He found my denial that I was not showing his copy to the opposition less than convincing, though technically the truth. After he rained on me a bit more, I suggested that he should wait until very near the copy deadline before bringing in his ads. He understood my meaning but did not spare me a rather lengthy and earthy lecture on the evils of Chestnut Ridge being a one newspaper town."

"Well, tell me, how did this titanic electoral struggle turn out?" Rocky asked, his curiosity overpowering his patience.

"Oh, the Republican won; the Democratic candidate, who, by the way, would have been no prize as a representative, ran third and the write in candidate ran second. In fact the write in total was a remarkable showing in a district where there had actually been no serious contest since the Civil War. He came very close to winning and might have if some Democrats would have crossed over. Their temptation to score a victory was so great that they voted for a lesser man than the former Republican incumbent who had served them well in a truly non-partisan fashion for fourteen years."

"So basically quite a few Republicans decided to vote for the man rather than for the party?"

"Yes," Brad said, smiling reflectively. "It was kind of heartening about the vitality of the democratic process. The fear-mongering about what would go wrong if one wrote in a name or used the stickers that were being distributed was incredible. The Republican campaign warned repeatedly that the stickers would fall off the ballot or that written in names would be disallowed if they weren't written precisely within the space. Voters were told that if so much as a letter of the name touched the edge of the box the vote would be invalid, which was rubbish, of course."

"So the university faculty didn't get to keep their friend in the legislature," Rocky mused.

"No, but they thought they got an even better friend into that legislative position two years later," smiled Brad.

"Really?" Rocky asked disbelievingly.

"Yes. They ran a faculty member as a Democrat in the next election, and he won. He was first Democrat legislator from this legislative district in one hundred and forty-two years."

"There has to be another story there," Rocky said expectantly as he noted Brad's reflective smile.

"It was the second time in two years that the legislative district witnessed a campaign unlike any it had seen in almost a century and a half, since the consequences of the war to preserve slavery entrenched the Republicans here as happened in many parts of the northern states. During that period, the liberalism of the party of Lincoln gradually turned into an entrenched laissez faire social and economic dogmatism while that same line of thought, which had dominated in the Democratic party, disappeared in favor of an energetic social and economic activism."

"Oh, my," chided Rocky with a feigned severity. "Am I hearing a manifestation of that liberal bias in the press?"

"You would be if I had had the guts to write like that when I was still writing local and national news rather than sports," Brad responded sheepishly.

Rocky looked sympathetic. "You're pretty hard on yourself. I'd like to hear why you returned to writing sports rather than other news, but tell me the story of that topsy turvy election first."

"Not surprisingly, the new Republican legislator from this district was of no consequence in Harrisburg. He had no seniority. His absolute loyalty to the minority party made it unnecessary for anyone to bargain for his vote, and there were already enough proponents for Christian conservatism in the legislature that there was little interest in having another one enter the already crowded field of speaking for that agenda.

"For those reasons plus the most important one, which is that an incumbent must win rather than lose elections, the local Democratic organization, whose sleepy, tenacious members were almost as uncomfortable with the unconventional behavior of academics as hide bound Republicans, accepted a faculty member from the state university as their party-endorsed candidate for the legislative seat. What they got for their compliance was the kind of campaign that they had never before put together. There were focus groups, district-wide voter surveys that revealed which neighborhoods to ignore during door-to-door campaigning and which to give maximum attention, and as vigorous a media campaign as they had mounted for the write-in candidate two years earlier."

"Proving once again that academics are just as zealous as right wing fanatics when their self-interest is at stake," Rocky said and shook his head in dismay. Suddenly he felt apologetic. "I'm sorry. I couldn't suppress that statement. It's a hangover from my reaction to the nineteen sixties, when academics projected an idealism that masqueraded the selfishness that really motivated them."

"No apology necessary," said Brad. "I'm a journalist, which is an occupation that requires a relentless effort to avoid cynical conclusions about the whole human race."

"I understand," Rocky said. "I'll try not to interrupt again."

"I hope you don't mean that," Brad responded agreeably and continued his story. "As I was saying, it was a vigorous and aggressive campaign, even more than the previous one because of there being only two combatants rather than the three of the previous election. Besides, it was also a national and state-level election year, so voter interest was greater than in a strictly local election year.

"Because of the national party involvement, even more money was being spent in another local contest as intensely disputed as the previous election. I was once again laying out more political advertising that would normally be the case. I fact, I was having daily ad copy submissions from the same two campaigners as in the last election. Mathew Carver was bringing in the Republican ads and Rufus Welty, who had worked in the write in campaign, was bringing in the Democrat ads."

"I suppose that Carver was getting to peak at the opponent's copy again," Rocky inferred.

"That became obvious very quickly. I asked the editor-in-chief how it could possibly be justified. He repeated the fairness argument of two years before, which I doubt if he believed himself. I pointed out that the Democrats surely knew what was happening. He responded that the election would not last forever and that the great majority of the paper's normal advertisers would concur with the concept of fairness that he had just stated. I wasn't to concern myself, he said. If anyone complained, I was merely to send them to him."

"So you were off the hook," Rocky concluded.

"If I wanted to be, I suppose, but," Brad paused reflectively, "I didn't want to feel relieved of responsibility."

"Ah, that troublesome conscience you inherited from your father was not subdued," Rocky said with a mixture of pity and amusement. "I suspect a tale of folly is about to be told."

Brad nodded acquiescence. "I'm not surprised that someone of your age and attainments has observed that folly and fairness are sometimes indistinguishable. The Democrats' ads were always submitted as close to deadline as they could. The managing editor was obviously holding space for the Republican side-by-side rebuttals later than the deadline I was bound to for my layout.

"To balance the situation, I secretly supplied the Democrats with the Republican copy that would appear in the paper, which came out at five o'clock. That gave them time to make the content of their radio and television ads for the afternoon a simultaneous response to whatever the content of the Republican ads in the paper were."

Rocky shook his head despairingly. "Thank God I wasn't living here. I'd have been between madness and boredom with the endless charges, rebuttals, rebuttals of rebuttals and so on."

"And all the campaigning through the media was all pointless," Brad stated. "The polls conducted throughout the campaign by the math professors who worked for the Democratic nominee showed that no more than a couple percent of change in preferring one or the other of the candidates from the beginning to the end of the campaign." The outcome resulted from one party's success in getting more of their voters to come to the polls on election day.

"And the outcome was what?" Rocky asked.

"The district got its first Democratic representative in one hundred and forty-two years," Brad answered. "Getting dozens of students to work on voter turnout was the factor that produced the democratic candidate's election for the first time in over a century despite the Republicans larger than two-to-one lead in the registration statistics."

"Quite a story."

"Yes," Brad nodded. "And it was the last one I wrote as a news reporter for this paper. I was assigned to sports and have been here ever since."

"Ouch," Rocky grimaced as though he had felt pain. "Your superiors must have found out about your undercover activities."

"Actually, they couldn't really prove it was me. There were several other plausible suspects. But the inference that it was me was likely enough that they made the change. Of course, they didn't give their suspicions as the reason for my re-assignment. They said that they needed to return me to sports because the sports coverage had deteriorated. I have enough pride in my former work in sports and enough exposure to the sports coverage since I'd left sports that I didn't contest the reason."

"I'm surprised that you weren't fired," Rocky opined.

Brad laughed heartily. "They weren't sure enough of themselves to try that. The rigors of the contest I'd have made really wouldn't have been worth their making the effort. My lawyer was salivating to get at them, even over the re-assignment."

"A real tiger, is he?"

"She," Brad corrected. "My wife. She's a partner in the biggest and most energetic law firm in town. She's very good."

Rocky eyed the son of his college friend with obvious admiration. "Have you never been tempted to try your hand at journalism elsewhere than here in Chestnut Ridge? You seem to know the business, and from the way you probed the story of Tank Robb's 'retirement,' you have the persistence and insight to do well in journalism anywhere, even in the so-called big time. Of course, from the way you restrained yourself in the case of Tank's story, I can see that you do have a streak of humanity that you'd have to suppress to be a success nationally as a reporter, but maybe you could overcome that unusual streak."

Brad smiled. "I'd like to think that, if I have no other attributes, I do have plain common sense. My wife is the big earner in our family. Annually, she makes anywhere from four to five times my salary. My salary just about, but not quite, covers our federal taxes. It wouldn't make sense for her to give up a partnership and become an associate in another firm for a fraction of her usual income even if I could triple my salary by going to some major market daily."

Rocky nodded his understanding of Brad's point. "My wife would sympathize with your dilemma. Her career was sacrificed to mine. That circumstance is a major unhappiness for thousands on thousands of professional women. It's not commonly a man's predicament." Rocky suddenly felt embarrassment. "I'm being insensitive. I didn't mean to impugn your masculinity."

Brad shook his head reassuringly. "No offense taken. I don't feel less manly because I live off my wife's earnings. I run into some men who think I'm something of a failure and others who admire me as some kind of enviable parasite.

"None of it really matters to me. It might if it affected the way our kids perceive me, but it doesn't seem to make a difference to them that dad makes less money than mom. I can tell you exactly when I gave any thought to the situation. One day I asked myself if there was anything that I had denied myself buying because my wife had earned the money rather than me. I realized that there wasn't. I haven't thought about the income difference since."

"At the risk of my being too personal, I wonder if the relationship between you and your wife is a typical one for what's called 'a happy marriage' these days?"

"We both know that a happy marriage is anything but typical these days," Brad responded with a chuckle. "But I'd say that we get along just fine. We're good to each other, and we have our share of laughs and disagreements."

Rocky could not avoid looking a bit mischievous. "So you don't follow the Golden Rule?" Rocky offered, his hand coming to his face and shielding his expression.

Brad responded with a laugh. "The Golden Rule? You mean the version that says, 'He who has the gold makes the rules?'" Brad shook his head decisively from side to side. "No, my wife isn't someone who says 'It's my money, we'll do it my way.' I have to confess, I wouldn't be able to handle that."

Rocky considered challenging Brad. He wanted to say that the younger man's description of his marital situation sounded too good to be true. Instead, he decided to change the subject. "Doesn't it bother you that you've never gotten out of writing sports or ever will?"

Brad looked pensive for a while before he responded. "It did for a little while when I first came back to it. But once I'd developed a detached perspective about the function of organized sports, both amateur and professional, it's been a source of enjoyment, admittedly sometimes a bit perversely."

Rocky was puzzled. "Isn't detachment the expected perspective of any reporter?"

"Not among sports writers," said Brad firmly. "They are as much consumers of the opiate as the public at large."

"The opiate?"

"You remember that Marx said that religion is the opiate of the people. I'm convinced that, if he were living in America now, he'd say that spectator sports is the opiate of the people."

"As a lifelong sports fan, I find that both vague and arguable, but if that's the case, why devote your professional life to writing about it?"

"I'm fascinated to see what forms the addiction takes," Brad said with a wry smile.

"Come on, Brad, people ought to be free to choose whatever recreation they want, and if they choose to be parked in front of the TV, so be it."

"You make it sound so harmless."

"Isn't it?"

Brad frowned and answered, "Do you know there's research that shows that people are depressed for a day or two after their favorite pro football team loses? Think of it," Brad said, his face showing a surrender to half-seriousness, "mass regional depression on Tuesday morning resulting from the outcome of Monday night football."

"At least that's not so serious as the behavior of soccer fans around the world," Rocky countered.

"Aren't you forgetting some of the destructive celebrations after championship outcomes in several of our professional sports? Of course, except for the violence against women, I admit that the destruction of property is not as bad in the long run as the attitude expressed by the mayor of Baltimore about the Ravens' super bowl victory."

"I'm afraid I didn't hear of it."

"He said to the city's super bowl victory celebrants, 'Aren't you glad we built a stadium instead of a museum?' That's an appalling revelation of the values that guide a major American city. I fear that the citizens of most American cities would make the same choice."

Rocky shook his head resignedly. "That's unusually extreme."

"Come on, Rocky, you know the sports situation in America is out of hand."

"I suppose you're going to make the usual speech about astronomical players' salaries, now," Rocky anticipated.

"I won't because I suspect you know as much about that absurdity as I do," Brad responded. "But while we are on the subject of money, I will argue that there is really no way to defend the cost that cities--none of which can provide a descent bus system--put themselves through to build stadiums to be torn down every thirty years or so."

"I concede that point; however, I will resort to my last line of defense. Watching professional sports is an integral part of our culture. The activity is defensible because it is an integral part of the fabric of our way of life. Just as the spectacles in the Coliseum were in Rome times. There would be an enormous recreational void if you could eliminate spectator sports tomorrow."

Brad smiled with challenging air. "That the fabric of the society has a flawed weave is a pathetic defense, if you'll excuse my bluntness. There are many other things--active things, healthful things--that people could do with their time."

Rocky saw an opening. "A person's recreation must be a choice. Don't go fascist on me, Herr Wright," Rocky chided.

"I know. That's why I don't write the opinions I've been talking about to you during this very pleasant interlude."

Rocky leaned back in his chair. He studied the journalist admiringly. Yet he was puzzled. "I understand--and even share--your feelings about the great misplaced value placed on sports and athletes in our culture, but how do you write sports without becoming a hypocrite?"

Brad responded immediately, seeming to state what was a well-established code of conduct in his mind. "I try my damedest to avoid writing of a game, the players, or a team as more important than it really is in the grand scheme of things. The superbowl isn't more important than the outcome of the game between the Eagles and the Giants in the local peewee football league, which itself is in danger of being thought to be overly important.

"As for the multi-million dollar athletes, I like to contribute what I can to portraying realistic limits of their abilities. For example, I was delighted to report that Michael Jordan, without question the greatest basketball player who ever lived, couldn't hit .300 as a minor league outfielder. To me that exemplifies the point that even the greatest of jocks are good at only their special thing. Similarly, a superb carpenter, who isn't going to make more than a fraction of Jordan's annual income in his entire life, is extraordinarily good at his particular thing. And of course, any rational person should know which of those two persons has more value to the society in the last analysis."

"So, you're going to spend the rest of your life writing sports for the consumption of us devotees of spectator sports?" Rocky concluded, his tone revealing his ambivalence at not being quite convinced that his own time spent as an enthusiastic fan of professional sports had been misguided.

Brad looked concerned that his had upset his father's old friend.

"If nothing else, writing sports has given me an appreciation of the irony that pervades life in general. It's not confined to the absurdity of jocks being lionized beyond the recognition given Noble laureates in the arts and sciences. You remember the story of the university faculty working and spending so heartily to send one of their number to the legislature? Six months into his term he voted to cut the university budget five percent."

Rocky was able to laugh openly at that. He got to his feet to leave. "Some how, you and I share a fundamental perception of what makes life tolerable. Enjoyment of irony is essential to livability." He shook Brad Wright's hand with genuine pleasure. "I am sorry we have not met sooner. I liked your father. You are a worthy successor."

"I'm proud to have you say that."

Rocky turned to go. "Oh, give my regards to your mother. And tell your wife she has my admiration, though we have never met."

Brad Wright smiled broadly as he raised his hand in farewell as Rocky left his office.

Chapter 7

Tony Rocco's visit with Brad Wright left him feeling a mixture of emotions. He was both satisfied and pleased that his lifelong perception of his admirable friend Dave Christiansen was, if anything, an under-appraisal. His wisdom, professional integrity, concern for the academic and personal welfare of children were well-established. Beyond that, his humanity, as shown in his protection of Portia Littleton and his salvaging a professional career for Tank Robb, was no less commendable for being subtly done. Rocky was prouder than ever to have counted him a friend.

At the same time, his discussion with Brad Wright about the journalist's marriage had proven unsettling. Though the man seemed perfectly happy in his relationship, he had compromised more to maintain the relationship than Rocky thought he himself could under similar circumstances. He did not think less of Brad Wright for having made the bargain with life that he had. He was distressed to think that he might not have been mature enough to handle such circumstances as Brad had. It reminded him that, although he had not indulged much in introspection since his retirement, he had been conscious throughout his working life that it was Beatrice who had made many and more significant compromises than he to maintain their marriage. He could not suppress the thought that his current unhappiness in marriage was selfish beyond reasonability. He struggled against the thought. He, like Brad Wright's wife, had been in a position to be the major earner in the family. This was not the case because of his having more ability than Beatrice but as the consequence of the development of circumstances. He had always felt that he need have no guilt over the direction of his marital relationship. Could he have been insensitive to the shift in that relationship that was inevitable since he and Beatrice had retired?

Rocky arrived at the motel where he and Beatrice were staying that night and where they would meet when she returned from her day of planning tomorrow's family gathering in a distressed state. He repeatedly told himself not to dwell on the disturbing question of his responsibility for the change in his marital relationship. No amount of mental gymnastics ever managed to put the feelings out of his mind completely that had led him to plan to flee his living situation.

Rocky worked for several hours on his eulogy before Beatrice returned to their motel room. Understandably, she was excited about the family gathering she had arranged for the next day. She recited to Rocky the plans that she and her cousin had made. They had reserved a shelter at a nearby state park and phoned relatives to alert them of the exact location of the event that they had been alerted to reserve time for several weeks before. A variety of food dishes to be brought by participants had been arranged for. Beatrice had committed herself to provide the wieners and burgers, so their next morning's preparations were scheduled to assure that they would be at the site before the others appeared shortly before lunch. Rocky was impressed, as always, by the thoroughness of Beatrice's planning. As his responsibilities for the next morning multiplied, he amused himself by playfully deriding her meticulousness. From long experience, he knew and appreciated that her sensitivity to pleasing guests made her entertainments the most thoroughly enjoyable that her guests were likely to experience unless they were provided with expensive catering.

For family events, Beatrice invariably exceeded even her normal meticulousness. Hence it was inevitable that during the next forenoon Rocky had two charcoal fires ready for cooking the ample supply of bratwurst, frankfurters and hamburgers before anyone else arrived for the family picnic. Before long, the relatives did begin to arrive: widowed aunts laden with salads or casseroles, young couples with armfuls of children and bags of fruit, cousins, some Beatrice's age and others one or two generations younger and lastly, and aged uncles carrying nothing but a conviction of the wisdom of every platitude that they would utter over the course of the day. Of the more than thirty people, Rocky had met perhaps half at one time or another and could recall perhaps a third of those. It was not, however, necessary to introduce himself, for he was familiar to all as Beatrice's husband. His recognition was confirmed by Beatrice's being the closest thing to a matriarch that was acknowledged in her family. It was, in fact, a family that had so many strong personalities that no one would acknowledge the pre-eminence of anyone else. This fact was the circumstance which explained the absence of some people who were at this moment not speaking to others in the family.

Rocky, who was not himself blessed with an extended family that he related to or who reached out to him, enjoyed the group. He was conscious that his ability to spend a full day spouting platitudes was second to no man's. Thus, while his politics and spiritual views could not be more opposite than those of the entire assemblage, he was confident that his day would not be unpleasant.

Of course, part of what kept Rocky out of conversational difficulty were the duties Beatrice assigned him as griller-in-chief. He had to tend the cooking of the meats with some care so that they would not all end fitting the extreme definition of well done that he preferred for himself. No that his assignment separated him from constant company. After all, every man who lived seemed firmly convinced that he knew better than anyone else how to cook over a charcoal fire. Rocky avoided irritation at such advice by injecting a generic derogatory statement about politicians. The fact that the comment was totally unresponsive to the cooking advice just uttered made no difference. Rocky's only conversational task for the next fifteen minutes his pro forma criticism of politicians would be to nod his head. He did not derive a sense of superiority from any of this; indeed he was entitled to none, because he was thoroughly enjoying himself. At least, he had been thus happily engaged, when Beatrice, who had been busy doling out paper plates, napkins and plastic utensils, while praising everyone's food contributions, cuddling babies and generally radiating amiability, approached Rocky as he was nursing the last of the meats they had brought. "Did you get enough to eat?" she asked.

"Plenty," Rocky assured her.

"Wasn't Aunt Frieda's macaroni salad especially good?" Beatrice enthused.

"Very good," Rocky agreed. "But of course, I liked the baked beans best."

"Always your favorite," Beatrice said. "I think you'd eat a fence post if I put enough barbecue sauce in it."

"That would perhaps be preferable to that green stuff you sent over. What exactly was it?"

"I'm not entirely sure myself," Beatrice responded. "Something bizarre was done to a perfectly innocent gelatin."

"That's a good description. Sounds like a criminal misdemeanor."

They stood silently for a while. Rocky fussed with the remaining hamburger and sausages, trying to keep them edible in case some late twinge of hunger would bring someone to request another. They both studied the pleasant surroundings. The lake they stood beside nestled between two heavily forested ridges. The water shimmering in the sun was being enjoyed by a number of canoeists and the swimmers and sunbathers at the beach on the opposite shore. The rest of their party were far enough away in the shade of the picnic shelter that the dominant sound was the whisper of a cooling breeze.

Beatrice looked up at Rocky and hesitantly asked, "Would you do something for me?"

"Of course," Rocky answered, expecting her to want him to do some task in preparation for the clean up which would begin in a couple hours when the first of the relatives would depart.

"I'd like you to talk to Marcia's Billy," said Beatrice, referring to the son of Beatrice's favorite cousin, Marcia Ashburn.

"Billy? It must be ten years since anyone's called him that," Rocky said. "'Billy' hardly suits a married man with a son who already looks like he'll one day match his father's height and athlete's build. That kid has to be one of the biggest ten year olds I've ever seen."

"You're right," Beatrice nodded. "I suppose I'm feeling so concerned for him that I resorted to thinking of him as we used to call him when he was a little boy."

"What's the problem?" Rocky asked, his interest immediately aroused. Twenty-nine year old Bill Ashburn was Rocky's favorite among the younger generation of Beatrice's extended family. He had married directly out of high school. With a wife and a child who came with the sometime haste of first born offspring, he wasted no time in becoming trained as a plumber and now had a thriving business that threatened to grow beyond what he could handle himself. Perhaps what Rocky enjoyed most about the young man was that his successful control of his life had not made him egocentric. His conversation was not deep, but he was an interested and aware observer of matters other than his personal concerns. Not the least of his charm was his willingness to ask questions of his conversant and to actually listen to the responses. Rocky would be genuinely sorry if the young man were now in serious difficulty. Rocky looked toward the picnic shelter, near which Bill and several other adults were playing catch with a gaggle of children. "It's money, I suppose. When young people have a problem it's usually about money," Rocky volunteered.

"Not this time," Beatrice said. "He and Karen are not getting along."

"Treece," Rocky sighed softly. "I am getting old and am probably not attuned to contemporary definitions. The vague phrase 'not getting along' is the number one problem with young married people, isn't it? I remember now how it was in our day, money was only conflict number two. If the old number 1 is still in the top spot, what can my talking to him do to help?"

"He needs to have a lot of patience with Karen, Rocky," Beatrice asserted. "You know, she moved out about a year ago."

"Yet she's here today," Rocky noted with puzzlement.

"Well, she moved back in about three months ago," Beatrice added.

"Sounds to me like the situation's working itself out, Treece," Rocky concluded. "You really think it's wise for a near total stranger to intrude at this point?"

"Bill's not happy, Tony. He needs some encouragement to be patient and keep trying to improve the relationship."

Rocky shook his head. "Beatrice, I'm not really the person to convince him of that. I've never been the shining example of patience myself, have I? Besides, what would his mother think? To have an outsider intruding into her son's life?"

"Marcia's the one who asked me to ask you to speak to Bill," Beatrice reported with finality.

Rocky shook his head. "She misjudges what my influence would be. She's always been close to Bill. I'm sure she's giving her son all the emotional support he can absorb."

"Marcia thinks that a man's point of view would help. She respects your judgment."

"Beatrice, Marcia's a widow, but she does have her father and three brothers who are closer kin to Bill than I am. Besides they've spent more time with him over the years than either of us have, you know."

"And yet she'd prefer that you speak to her son," Beatrice observed.

"Do it, please. Really, Tony, I wish you would."

Rocky studied his wife's earnest face. Not only would the task be incredibly awkward to initiate, but it would be fruitless, he believed. But the conviction he heard in Beatrice's desire to have him speak comfortingly to the young man whom he genuinely liked and would help if he could overcame his resistance. "I probably won't even be able to get him alone to talk. But if I can, I'll talk to him about it," Rocky conceded.

Leaving Beatrice to keep the remaining grilled meats to avoid their reduction to cinders before someone would claim them, Rocky walked over to the game of catch, where a mixture of adults and older children had formed a circle inside which stood a number of smaller children who were energetically trying to intercept the softball that was being thrown back and forth across the circle. Of course, throws were arched temptingly close to the little arms and hands that stretched upward that always found the ball just out of reach before it lodged in the hands of an adult recipient on the edge of the circle. Rocky stood near Bill and watched the tossing for a while. Bill noticed his presence after a bit and offered to make a place for him in the circle of players.

Rocky declined to be included, but an idea for pursuing his task struck him. Rocky said that he was about to go for a short walk and asked Bill if he would like some accompany him. Bill expressed his pleasure at the prospect of joining his older relative. The young man said that he would tell Karen to keep an eye on their son Billy, who was one of the youngsters inside the circle, and trotted off toward the picnic shelter. As Rocky watched Bill speak briefly to the tall attractive woman that he knew to be the young man's estranged wife, he felt ambivalent that his artless tactic to get Bill alone for a conversation had succeeded. Pleading the absence of opportunity to Beatrice would have made his situation for the rest of the picnic immeasurably easier, he was sure.

Rocky and his nephew walked silently for a short time. Rocky began the conversation by inquiring about the state of Bill's plumbing business. Bill briefly responded that he had an abundance of work, cooperative suppliers and promptly paying customers. Another period of silence ensured. Then Rocky said, "Well, I guess I'd say that you don't have a worry in the world, except that I know better."

Bill stopped walking and looked at the older man blankly. Perhaps he was considering pretending that he didn't know to what Rocky was referring. Then he said, "I suppose that someone's been talking to you about Karen and me."

Rocky paced a few steps slowly to draw Bill into continuing their walk. "It's impossible for word of your situation not to spread," Rocky said.

"Maybe so," Bill admitted, "but I'd rather not have people talk about it."

"Some discuss it because they love gossip, but others because they care about you," said Rocky. "Be grateful for that, as distressing as it seems at times."

"It's embarrassing," Bill said, his head bowed as they trudged on, their pace reflecting the dreariness of the subject being discussed. "I know that some of the cousins think a guy's not much of a man if his wife leaves him."

"You know better than to take that kind of talk seriously," Rocky scoffed. "What reason did she give when she left?"

"She said that little Billy and I were holding her back. She had to get on her own."

"Did she say what she was being held back from?"

"No. I thought she was happy. She was back in school getting her masters in business. She was up for promotion at her company when she left. She's gotten it and the degree since."

Rocky hesitated before he asked, "Is or was there another man?"

"No," Bill nodded, continuing his reluctance to look Rocky in the face. "There was a guy she spent a lot of time with, but it turned out he was gay."

"So she's back now?"

"Yeh, finally," sighed Bill. "She first wanted to come back about six months after she left, but I didn't agree at that time."

"You weren't sure you wanted her back?"

"No, I wanted her back. I always have," Bill admitted wistfully. "But she insisted on some conditions at that time that I couldn't accept. She has this girl friend that she wanted to bring back with her to our house on condition they'd live with me and Billy that but she and I wouldn't be together."

Rocky stopped and peered at his young nephew. "She's become a lesbian? And she wanted you to provide a nest for her and her lover in the house where you were man and wife?"

Bill shook his head vigorously. "No, that wasn't it. The woman was truly just a friend. Karen wanted her in the house as a buffer between us. She was still saying that marriage had held her back. She was willing to live at home as a friend but with no intimacy between us."

Rocky gestured acceptingly toward the young man. "I'm glad you didn't accept that arrangement."

"Well," Bill began hesitantly, "I now kind of have. That's why she came back last month."

"With her girl friend?"

"No, no girl friend," Bill responded quickly, followed by some hesitancy before adding, "but no intimacy with me either."

Rocky shrugged his shoulders acceptingly, "Well, it's not surprising that it would take some time to get back to normal."

Bill looked at Rocky eye to eye for the first time. "The way it is now is as normal as it's going to be."

Rocky looked disbelievingly. "No intimacy? Ever?"

Bill studied the tops of the trees that shaded the path that they were walking and nodded affirmatively.

"So you're not getting a divorce, or a legal separation, or--what am I thinking--you can't get a separation if you're living under the same roof." Rocky looked at Bill with shocked disbelief. "Why are you doing this?"

Bill picked up a stone and sent it off into the trees. "Mom says that Karen will come around. That I should be caring without being aggressive and that things will work out."

Rocky smiled, "*Work out,* huh? I wonder what that means in this instance? Let me guess," Rocky asserted. "You're handling all the living expenses and, of course, putting a roof over Karen's head, and you're looking after your kid plus making all the effort to mend the relationship. Oh, and one more thing: you're making no demands. Right?"

Bill hesitated before he answered. "Yeh, that's so. But I don't care about money. I want things to get back the way they were before she left."

Rocky raised his eyebrows skeptically. "You mean sharing responsibilities, sex, the whole package?"

"Yes," Bill said forlornly.

Rocky shook his head in dismay. "Bill, things will never get back to how they were then."

"You don't think so?"

Rocky's mouth pursed into an expression of rejection. "Not a snowball's chance in hell."

"Lots of couples get though something like this," Bill insisted.

Rocky's head shook in disagreement. "I don't think they do. Maybe you're thinking of people with definitive sexual identities who make it up after one of them has been unfaithful. I don't say I could myself, but I don't contest that some people do, or seem to, though from what I've seen they no longer need refrigeration to keep the food cold. But I concede that situation has more of a chance to be overcome than yours does.

"If you're convinced that you know the truth, that there never was another guy and that her female friend isn't a lover, then Karen just plain doesn't want to be married. Seems to me you're making that possible while subsidizing her independence. She wanted to bring someone to be the wall between you. I'm glad you didn't stand for that, Bill, but there is still a wall, from what I'd guess."

"It's uncomfortable, I admit."

Rocky snorted. "You have a gift for understatement. You can't endure this situation and be happy."

"I can handle it if it's not forever," Bill said resignedly.

"Bill, you're just postponing an even bigger pain in the future. "

"You think there's no chance it will get better?"

Rocky is perplexed that Bill wanted to hang on to a relationship which promised continuous pain and an inevitable trauma. He realized that he had been foolish to actually give explicit advice, but he was outraged at what he considered a situation where a fine young man was being grossly used. "Bill, you are eventually going to be presented with divorce papers. Your choice is to present yours to her now or get some from her later after a lot more unhappiness. I think you should do it now. You're trying to salvage something that doesn't exist any more. Besides, you're in the fortunate position of knowing that your wife has shown she has no interest in taking your son."

"Mom'd be so disappointed if I filed for divorce."

Rocky responded earnestly. "I can't believe your mother would want you to live in an endlessly painful situation. She always wants what's best for you."

Bill studied the ground for a time and chose not to respond to Rocky's prediction of his mother's reaction to his divorcing Karen. "We'd better start back." He had nothing further to say for the twenty minutes of their return walk back to the picnic shelter.

On arrival back at the shelter, they found the group awash in either bantering amusement or consternation. The cause of this situation was Bill Ashburn's ten year old son Billy who sat impatiently and noisily in a canoe some seventy feet off shore shouting for assistance that was not being initiated, let alone on the way. It was explained to Rocky and Bill that the boy had decided, without permission or the accompaniment of an experienced paddler, to try his hand at an excursion on the lake with his father's canoe.

Unfortunately, the paddle had slipped out of his grasp and he was now adrift, his efforts to propel the canoe shoreward with swings of one arm in the water while he clutched the side of the canoe with the other had not resulted in any progress. Since the boy was in no danger, his predicament was being viewed more with amusement than concern. The adults were aware that they could go to the boat rental facility on the opposite shore and get a boat for a rescue if the situation had passed the point of amusement.

Bill, not surprisingly, did not share the general amusement at his son's situation. His glanced toward where his wife sat. Her apparent unconcern with her son's dilemma was evident in her attention being focused on the book she was reading. Bill looked from Karen to the pile of floatation vests brought with the canoe and to his son, who was not wearing one. After another angry glance at Karen, Bill muttered to Rocky that he did not know what had gotten into Billy lately.

Bill pulled off his shirt, and took off his shoes and socks. He walked to the shore and asked the boy if he could see the paddle. Satisfied with the boy's response that the paddle was floating not far away on the side of the canoe opposite from the shore where his father stood, Bill swam out to the paddle. He handed it into the boat. Then positioning the boy in the spot that gave the best stability, he rolled up into the canoe and soon had the craft and his son, who endured continuous chastisement while his father paddled, ashore.

Except for Bill, the assemblage found the event and its harmless outcome the topic that enlivened conversation until the picnic declared itself ended with the series of departures, each of which was lengthy, as people took leave of relatives they might not see for some time afterward. As the nearest thing to hosts of the event, Rocky and Beatrice handled the final details of cleaning up and were the last to leave. Rocky noted the sullenness that clouded Bill Ashburn's face every time he looked at his wife until the unhappy looking pair departed. The amiability and attention that Bill showed toward his son made clear whom he held responsible for his son's misadventure with the canoe.

Rocky found Beatrice strangely silent during their ride back to the motel. He had expected her to be talkative, considering her pleasant day with relatives she liked and did not get to see very often. Rocky's day had not been unpleasant, albeit his enthusiasm for the people at the picnic was no where near Beatrice's. "Not a bad day," he offered to Beatrice, whose engrossment with the roadside scenery seemed inordinately intense.

Beatrice was slow in answering and then turned to him and offered with disgust, "I can't believe that you did what you did today."

Rocky was surprised. He could not immediately think of any indiscretion he had committed. Of course, he knew from past experience that occasionally some action or statement that he considered innocent or innocuous was offensive to Beatrice. He had decided long ago that the sensible course of action was to apologize rather than defend himself. After all, he recognized that injury was in the feelings of the injured, not the logic of the unintentional perpetrator. "Whatever it was, I meant no injury to whomever I offended. I'm sorry."

"It's not me that's owed an apology. And, at this point, I doubt an apology would fix anything. God, I can't believe you'd do such damage so thoughtlessly."

"Hey, wait now, this sounds very serious," Rocky interposed. "I can't think of what I might have done that has such serious consequences." At that moment, they had arrived at the motel, and he was unable to look at Beatrice as he looked for a parking spot.

Beatrice looked at Rocky with anger glinting from her narrowed eyes. "I can't believe you are as obtuse as you sound. It was just plain insensitive. Not a new trait for you unfortunately," Beatrice fired at him as she got out of the car and shut the door forcefully.

They were in their room before any further dialogue. "Are you going to tell me what it is I've done, or not?" asked Rocky.

Beatrice's frustration was palpable as she faced him belligerently. "If you insist on my stating the obvious, you were asked to advise Billy to be patient with Karen and instead you told him he ought to divorce immediately."

Rocky's spirits sank with the recognition that he had, in fact, misperceived the task he had been given. He had assumed that he had been asked to give Bill Ashburn his best judgment about what he should do about his marital situation. He remembered now that he had been asked specifically to counsel patience and endurance. On hearing the actual details of Bill's situation, Rocky had advised his nephew in accord with what he would do himself in a similar situation. That was definitely not what the young man's mother and Beatrice had wanted done.

Rocky felt contrite, not because he thought his advice unwise, but because it was contrary to what Bill's mother wanted. Had he known before hand the specific circumstances of Bill's situation, or had he listened more closely to what had been asked of him, he would have refused to talk to Bill at all. "I see now that I did wrong. I thought I was supposed to tell him what I thought was the best course of action. When I heard how Karen's using him, my sincere judgment is that he shouldn't tolerate the situation. I honestly believe no amount of patience will change that into a happy marriage. That woman will always make him miserable, not to mention the negative impact that I think the situation's having on their son."

Beatrice stood by impatiently while Rocky unlocked their motel room door. "Since when did you become the master psychologist? And to offer a diagnosis on such scanty information, too. So impressive." Although Beatrice was almost never sarcastic, she managed it in depth with her last statement.

"O.K., you're right," Rocky conceded. "I should have kept my opinion to myself. Or better still, I should have kept out of it altogether. I'm sorry."

Beatrice put down her purse and paced back and forth a few moments, then began to move their belongings around for no particular reason. Finally she paused and said, "I'll need some time to settle down. I'm going down to the bar to have a drink. Don't come down for a while."

Rocky occupied himself with a half hour of surfing the television channels pausing for brief glimpses at programs he was barely attentive to, neither when he came to them nor when he left them. Then he showered and changed clothes. Beatrice reacted to his arrival in the bar by remembering her own desire to shower and change before dinner. Hence it was another hour before they were seated in the dining room for a meal that was eaten during a series of widely spaced, terse comments on mundane subjects that failed to qualify as a real conversation.

It was an emphatic indication of Beatrice's wanting to comfort herself that, when asked by the waitress if she wanted dessert, she asked for a cream sherry. The sweet sherry was an indulgence of hers for encouraging or perpetuating a tranquil mood. When the waitress had set the glass of amber liquid before her and departed, Beatrice said, "I shouldn't have asked you."

Rocky was mixing in just the right proportions the tea and brandy he had ordered before adding a half-teaspoon of raw sugar, thus creating his own favorite soporific. He felt sincerely contrite and said, "I should have listened more carefully to your request and done what I was asked to do." He paused to stir his fortified tea and added, "but, to be honest, Treece, I don't think I gave him bad advice. Doesn't Bill's mom see how that woman is using her son?"

"She sees, and she's anguished over it."

"Bill's too fine a man to have to continue in this aggravating situation, which I truly believe will never change. Did you see the absolute lack of concern she exhibited when her son was stranded on the lake without a paddle?"

"Believe me, Tony, Marcia is greatly distressed over Billy's situation. But, unlike you, she's convinced that in the long run it's best for him to try to save his marriage. Marcia thinks her daughter-in-law will eventually see that marriage is not incompatible with the other things she wants to do with her life."

"Surely she should have seen that by now if she still loved Bill. In the mean time, Bill gets to have a non-contributing boarder and major sexual frustration, not to mention some severe damage to a quite normal masculine ego." Rocky shook his head in dismay. "The man deserves better."

"See," Beatrice smiled wryly, "it's that 'masculine ego' thing that shouldn't be getting in the way. I hope you didn't give that as the reason that he should divorce Karen--that his manhood was being challenged."

"I don't think that I put it quite like that, but I won't deny that might have been in the back of my mind. Truthfully, I don't think it's irrelevant. I think we are all--male and female--entitled to a healthy ego. Besides, Treece, why apply any complex psychology to the situation? She doesn't want him; she's clearly enough shown it. Surely any man with defensible self-respect would walk away walk away, taking the kid that she already has shown that she thinks is a burden."

"Ah, ha" Beatrice nodded, "there's a revelation. You suggested to Billy that he walk away. No surprise. Walking away is your standard tactic for dealing with marital problems."

Rocky was alarmed by Beatrice's assertion. "How did this suddenly get to be about us?"

"Maybe it ought to be about us."

"Why?" Rocky asked, though he did not want an answer. The question was the first thing to come to mind as he desperately sought a way to deflect a discussion he did not want to pursue. His guilt was irrepressible. After all, if the escape plan that he considered merely delayed had been acted on as planned, he would have deserted his marriage five days ago without explanation to Beatrice.

Beatrice's eye contact was piercing. "There are more ways to walk away than doing so literally," she said pointedly. "Just not talking about your feelings is your favorite one of them."

Rocky struggled against his defensive feelings. "That's no doubt true at times. But I believe those instances are a fraction of the number of times a problem would have been exacerbated by lengthy discussion of it. I'll bet that Bill and Karen have done plenty of talking about their situation, and what good has it done?"

"It may be too soon to tell. Besides, if it doesn't work out, at least they tried," Beatrice offered.

"Look," Rocky began with notable intensity, "we should drop this subject. We'll only get upset to no purpose. I apologize for what I said to Bill. I'll apologize to his mother if you want me to."

Beatrice looked at her husband resignedly. "O.K., maybe you're right. There's no point in discussing it with regard to us. As to the other thing, talking to Marcia might just make things worse. I'm ready to call it a day." Rocky was greatly relieved as he joined Beatrice in leaving the lounge and starting toward their room.

When they entered their room, the flashing light on the phone alerted them that they had received a message. Rocky called the motel desk and was told that Andrew Trumbull had called and wanted the Roccos to return the call this evening. The call led to a convoluted speculative dialogue between the Roccos, the complicated nature of which pushed their recent tense discussion of their relationship into the background. The Trumbulls were another couple from the area that the Roccos had known since their college days. Rocky and Beatrice had had then and continued to this day to have a paradoxical relationship with them.

Andrew and Martha Trumbull were both amiable and yet not always a joy to be around. There were two reasons that the time spent with them was not an unalloyed pleasure. The Trumbulls never spent more than a couple hours together with other people without at least one extended exchanging verbal barbs with each other. They never had a dialogue that qualified as a full-blown spat, but never were they far from their next comment on one another's shortcomings as a spouse or failings as a housemate. They had nothing of interest in common except a joint enthusiasm for their grown children. The Roccos and the rest of their circle of college friends recognized that the Trumbulls now having one topic they agreed on was an improvement over the relationship of their college years. Then, the Trumbulls had nothing in common except a consuming interest in physical passion, which was, after all, an interest shared by their entire age group.

The Roccos knew that the Trumbulls now each had separate interests that each pursued intensely. Martha enjoyed the arts. Since Andrew was as likely to enter a museum or a theatre as he was to journey to the far side of the moon, Martha visited such places with regularity with female friends. Andrew's passions were playing golf and bowling, two activities that Martha viewed with the enthusiasm of a dieter who was offered a limp stick of celery. Andrew was passionate not only about playing the two sports themselves, but was continuously involved with the organizations available to amateur participants in the two sports. In fact, Andrew served on the state level boards of the organizations for amateur golfers and amateur bowlers.

At its best, Andrew's conversation about his devotion to his two favorite sports never reached the level of tolerable entertainment. Martha, on the other hand, could say something one could listen to without struggling to fake interest if she could be led to discussing the aesthetics of the paintings she had recently viewed in museums or the content of the plays she had recently attended. The monologue was less that enthralling if she focused exclusively on the comfort and complexity of the journey, the amenities at the theatre or museum and the meals consumed during the trip. With Andrew, the hope was for brevity, for he seemed never to grasp that someone else's enthusiasm for the politics of amateur sports associations or the exploits of unknown amateur golfers and bowling teams was very limited. With Martha there was hope of an interesting conversation if one was an adroit questioner.

The Roccos occasionally asked themselves why they still felt friendly feelings toward the Trumbulls. They recognized that the pair were warm human beings whose bickering had since lost any element of rancor and was now a ritual of maintaining a relationship rather than wanting to wound or trying to effect change in the other spouse. Sometimes, in fact, it seemed they were performing a playlet for the amusement of their listeners. The question was always whether or not one was in the suitable mood to enjoy this theatre of the absurd.

"You know if we call them they'll want to spend the day," Rocky warned.

"Oh, right," Beatrice sighed, rejecting Rocky's note of concern. "You couldn't stand playing golf tomorrow. You know that's what he always wants to do."

Rocky seized the opportunity for some lightheartedness to put away the tension of the last several hours. Ensuring that his voice and demeanor radiated a false concern, he said, "I'm only thinking of you. What would you do with yourself if Andy and I spent the day playing golf?

Beatrice joined in the spirit of Rocky's effort. "You're so considerate," she said with melodramatic insincerity. "I know that Martha's unaccustomed to venturing out of the nest without Andrew, but perhaps she will make an exception and think of somewhere we can fill the time until the return of our brave protectors."

"I suspected you'd bear up," Rocky admitted. "Of course, Andy's not going to be much of a source for material for the eulogy, and tomorrow's my last chance to get some additional perspective."

"It's up to you whether we call them or not," Beatrice responded. "Martha's company is always a mixed blessing. Realistically, we can't not return the call and explain ourselves to them at the reunion the day after tomorrow."

Rocky decided that Beatrice's logic was unassailable. He made the call and found the invitation to spend the day was just as anticipated. Rocky weakly pleaded the necessity of further pursuit of his task; Beatrice spoke with Martha and had to admit that she had no plans for visiting family the next day. They agreed to meet the Trumbulls for breakfast before the men proceeded to the Andy Trumbull's country club and the women decided among several the possibilities for spending the day that Martha had suggested.

Chapter 8

Because the directions that Rocky had written down for getting to the restaurant for breakfast with the Trumbulls had turned out not be as clear as hoped for, the Roccos were fifteen minutes late in arriving at the only restaurant in the small town where the Trumbulls lived. They were pleased to find the large dining room cheerful both in appearance and clientele; however, their friends were not to be seen. The Roccos had been seated and were into their second cups of coffee when the Trumbulls appeared. After a round of effusive greetings and exchanging assessments about looking well, which were not much of an exaggeration for either couple, Andrew Trumbull apologized for their being late and asserted the cause to be Martha's ever-increasing slowness.

"You remember how she was always late for everything--classes, dances, whatever? At the rate she's going, she'll miss her own funeral."

Martha looked smug and picked up her menu, "I'll be there for yours, Andy, never fear. And I'll wear something appropriate to the celebration." Martha smiled across the table and said, "I don't suppose he'll mention how much time he wasted going back for his precious golf cap after we were half way here."

"Hey," Andy chided, "its got Jack Nicklaus's autograph of the inside. I wanted Rocky to see it."

Rocky was disappointed to see that his friend had succumbed to the current fashion of men wearing hats indoors. "Well, let's have a look at it," said Rocky as he reached out for Andy to hand him the cap he was wearing.

"Oh, I don't wear it, Rocky, I just brought it for you to see," Andy explained. Andy frowned and said, "Damn," he grumbled with frustration, "I left it in the car."

Martha displayed a pleased smile. "At least that spares the locals another look at it. When he unveils it, be very careful handling it, Tony," Martha counseled with melodramatic exaggeration. "It's designated for our son in Andy's will."

"So I guess you won't be loaning it to me to play golf today, Andy," Rocky grinned mischievously.

Martha smiled broadly and Andy began to offer a defense of his reverence for the cap but stopped in mid statement as the waitress arrived to take their orders.

Until the arrival of the food, the men were largely silent as Martha listed for Beatrice some possibilities for how they might spend their day. Martha's strongest recommendation was that they visit the factory showroom of a nearby metalworking forge that did artistically designed hammered bronze and aluminum plates, trays and memorabilia. Beatrice was familiar with the company's work since it was found in better gift shops on the west coast. She liked some pieces she had seen in their retail shops but had resisted buying any for herself although she's given the work as gifts; therefore, shopping at the factory store was her first choice of how to spend the day. Andy pleaded that Beatrice should not let Martha delude herself that the items would be much cheaper at the factory. He professed relief that they were not more expensive than retail there because Martha lacked all restraint in shopping.

Lack of restraint in shopping was a well-worn topic between the Trumbulls and Martha responded to Andrew's accusation without annoyance. She told Beatrice that she was not to worry because there was plenty of room in the trunk and back seat of their car so neither one of them would have to restrain themselves in making purchases today.

"Whoa, wait," Andy countered, "you're not going to have our car. Rocky and I are taking that to the club."

"Don't be silly, Andy," Martha responded, "you and Tony can use the rental they're driving. I need the sedan."

Andy shook his head in refusal. "That's tough. I guess you shouldn't have sent your car to the garage. I told you to wait. As usual you wouldn't listen."

"That's irrelevant and you know it, Andy. I'm sure Tony won't mind driving to the golf course, will you, Tony?"

The arrival of the four plates piled high with food momentarily delayed Rocky's answer. They had all begun to eat when Rocky said, "I don't mind driving to the golf club, besides, I think you ladies would find our rental a bit too crowded. It's a compact, and we have the trunk and part of the back seat full of luggage."

Beatrice could not resist a playful injection into the dialogue. "Based on what I'm expecting to buy, Martha, I'm afraid there'd be no room in the compact rental for you to make any purchases."

Andy clapped his hands. "That would be the best break I've had in a while."

"Yes," said Martha, "and it would be the last one you'd have for a long time, Mr. Trumbull."

Andy's resistance to yielding what he emphatically described as 'his' car continued throughout the meal. When Martha finished her coffee, she asked Beatrice if she had finished her breakfast. On receiving an affirmative response, she said, "Well, Tony, I guess you'll have to give Treece the keys to the rental car."

Rocky handed over the keys with some embarrassment. He really thought it was sensible for the women to have the more comfortable car since they would be doing considerably more driving; however he saw no point in debating the matter with Andy Trumbull. He looked up a minute or two later in surprise as Beatrice re-entered the restaurant and approached the table. She smiled broadly and said, "Gentlemen, you will need these keys if you're going to get to the golf course." She set the keys to the rental car down on the table. "And, Rocky, here's the autographed cap. Martha thinks you'll need protection from the sun." She drew the cap from behind her back and put it on the table beside the keys.

Andy looked more puzzled than angry. "Where is that woman?" he asked.

"She's in your car with the motor running. She says that if you go out the door she'll drive away."

Andy shook his head resignedly before his face adopted a wry grin. "I didn't even know she had keys for that car." Rocky thought Andy looked like a fighter who had been ahead on points until the last round and lost the fight on a knock out. Of course, considering the marital relationship of the Trumbulls, a re-match would not be too long in coming. Rocky reflected that at least he had been spared marriage as an endless succession of contests for supremacy.

Rocky noted that Andy was not out of sorts during the drive to his country club. Nor did he verbalize on what manner of retaliation he would exact from Martha at his earliest opportunity. In fact, the few references he made to his wife before they began their round of golf contained a kind of admiration for her adroitness in besting him that morning.

Andy's demeanor was puzzling for Rocky. Of course, he would not have engaged in a contest with Beatrice over a choice of cars in similar circumstances. However, had he had a conflict with Beatrice over some minor matter, he would be seething now instead of behaving as amiably as Andy was at the moment. He would be hours returning to tranquility while Andy seemed not to have been discomforted at all by his disagreement with his wife. While he was grateful that he and Beatrice did not have the sort of contentious relationship that the Trumbulls did, he envied the apparent absence of residual animosity in Andy and, presumably, in Martha.

Rocky could not imagine Andy planning a disappearance as he himself had planned. Had he not been frustrated from disappearing for the time being because of the task he had been given for the reunion and Beatrice's unexpectedly accompanying him of the trip, he would have disappeared by now. It was perhaps in emulation of Andy that he made an effort to put all grave matters out of mind and devote the day exclusively to the enjoyment of a game of golf.

While Andy attended to the details of obtaining his guest pass and a pair of shoes to use, he directed Rocky toward the first tee while he got a riding cart, his own clubs and a set for Rocky to use. Rocky sat on a bench near the first tee and enjoyed the attractiveness of the manicured rolling terrain with its defining trees that created an impressive playing terrain for the golfers. As he studied the thick carpet of grass on the first tee and down the first fairway, Rocky marveled that Andy had such a beautiful, well-kept facility to play so frequently as such modest cost. He thought of the people in urban areas such as where he lived who either played on hard and poorly grassed courses or paid astronomically higher memberships than Andy did to enjoy an occasional round of golf on a well-kept course with attractive amenities. He was amazed that such quality of play and other pleasantries could be available at such moderate cost. Though his skills as a golfer were modest and he would likely be exploring the rough that bordered the lush fairways, he was looking forward to a very pleasant day.

That expectation was dissolved when Andy drove up in the cart and announced that they would be joined on their round of golf by Dwight Kensington. Rocky turned away from his friend of four decades and saw the green landscape as a blur. His annoyance at the very thought of Kensington returned as strongly as he had felt it when he first experienced it during his junior year in college. Even if Kensington had not distressed the hypersensitive collegian that was Anthony Rocco in two specific instances, his general deportment was an irritant. Merely what Kensington was and how he behaved affronted Rocky, a youth of humble origins and slender means. Kensington was an atypical enrollee at the state university. He was from an affluent and prominent family and was a student at Glassport State as a kind of penance. The former teachers college that had only recently diversified to an undergraduate arts and sciences institution largely drew its student body from offspring of immigrants or a subsequent generation or two. Predominantly, they were the first of their families to pursue higher education. Dwight Kensington was definitely not from that milieu. His family had been in America long enough to pretend they had never immigrated. He was the only member of his family who had not enrolled at a prestige private university for his education.

Though Dwight Kensington was not lacking in intelligence, his academic record in prep school had been so poor, he could not be admitted to the kind of university that his family would normally have in mind for him. This troubled Dwight not in the least. At

Glassport State, he was the largest fish in the pond. In the post World War II era when Kensington and Rocky were college contemporaries, it was rare for any student, even military veterans with a family living in college housing, to have a car. Kensington drove a new convertible of a higher-priced make. When most students nursed meager funds for an occasional movie, Kensington did not need to let economics dictate his social life. It was fortunate that he was not predatory, for his social opportunities were considerably more numerous than those of any other male on campus.

Rocky could have largely ignored Kensington the social animal except for an occasional twinge of male hormonal jealousy. However, in two specific episodes, Dwight Kensington become a major annoyance to the young and volatile Anthony Rocco. In college, Rocky's greatest joy beyond his studies was playing end on the college football team. His presence as a starter was principally accorded on the basis of his defensive aggressiveness and his offensive blocking ability. However, his lack of height and mediocre speed prevented him from being an outstanding contributor as a pass receiver despite his being able to catch the ball very well. In those days, platoon football had almost eliminated a chance to play both offense and defense, but Rocky performed well enough to get playing time in both phases of the game, even though the volatile Rocky had never been a favorite with the coach because of his mercurial behavior.

That lack of fondness that the coach had for Rocky no doubt contributed to the coach's desire to diminish Rocky's role when the tall, classically built Dwight Kensington appeared at the start of Rocky's senior season. Though Kensington made clear that baseball was his favorite sport and the one he intended to compete in at Glassport, he looked to the football coach like the model specimen of a offensive end compared to the five foot nine inch Anthony Rocco. The coach encouraged Kensington to try being a pass catching end. Indeed, he was an adequate receiver and was a bit faster than Rocky. Of course, he was easier for the passer to see down field. That he was a less than mediocre blocker compared to Rocky did not trouble the coach who preferred to have the bigger target for the passing game. By mid-season Rocky got no playing time with the offense even though Dwight's poor blocking was a liability to the running game.

Rocky was even getting less playing time with the defense because he was now in competition with players whose role had always been confined to defense. His designation as a starting player had ended.

Rocky, who was never capable of suffering in silence, began to vent his frustration on opposing players with whom he came into contact on the rare occasions when he played and on his teammates who opposed him in practice scrimmages. The coach's lectures on sportsmanship only resulted in increasing Rocky's sullenness. Finally, Rocky's aggressive confrontation in practice with another player earned him a short suspension from the team. Rocky bridled at the harshness of the penalty, since he had not initiated the incident yet was held solely to blame. Rocky returned to the team for a short time after his suspension, but he soon had a violent verbal exchange with the coach which ended his career as a college football player.

Somewhat irrationally, Rocky's bitterness over the loss of an activity that had been a great joy to him focused on a student manager who had taunted Rocky with an imitation of one of the football coach's lectures to Rocky on sportsmanship. Rocky irrationally vented his anger at the student's lighthearted jibe when he could not at the coach who clung to his preference for playing Kensington over him even when the objective data suggested that he should abandon his experiment. The episode only exaggerated Rocky's already well-established reputation for wildness, even among students who had never seen such behavior from him. He lost both his athletic activity and the potential good will of many students who were strangers to him.

An event occurred during Rocky's last semester in school that heightened his distaste for Kensington even though the rancor over the football disappointment had begun to fade as Rocky looked ahead to a career and adult independence. During one of the periodic hiatuses in the romance between Rocky and Beatrice, which was usually the result of Rocky's feeling a lack of enthusiasm for him in the woman he had already fixed on as a lifetime partner, Dwight Kensington began to date Beatrice. No alpha male of a wolf pack ever responded with greater intensity than did Anthony Rocco at his learning who his adored one's dating partner was. The only thing that saved Dwight Kensington a fistfight was Rocky's conviction that any chance he had of ever re-establishing a relationship with Beatrice depended on his not physically confronting Dwight Kensington. It was small wonder that Rocky had been pleased to never see Dwight Kensington again after graduating from Glassport State.

Emerging from a distasteful reverie, Rocky darted an annoyed look at Andy Turnbull. "Damn it, Andy," Rocky grumbled, "why did you ask him along? You know how I feel about the guy."

"Relax Rocky. I need to get next to Dwight to do a little business. I'm going to ask him to underwrite a big piece of the cost of the annual club championship tournament next month. His pockets are deeper than ever; you'd be surprised what a good business man he's been.

"Help me out with this, Rocky. Don't give him the cold shoulder, please. Besides you're not going to have to get very close to him. He's going to ride with me in one cart and you will use this one alone." Andy gestured toward the back of the cart. "See. The only clubs on this cart are the ones I rented for you. Dwight is bringing mine and his on the cart he's driving. Don't worry. Just enjoy your round."

Rocky pondered a response to Andy's request as he began to examine the rental clubs, but before he said anything, Andy spoke again. "Oh, one more thing, Rocky. I think that you knew the girl that Dwight married right after he graduated. Don't ask about her, please. They went through a break up that was very hard on Dwight. It's a sore subject that he doesn't like to be reminded of. All of the Glassport State gang avoid mentioning it when Dwight's around. Play along, will you? I want him in a good frame of mind when I hit him up for major funding for the club tournament this year."

"Maybe you'd like me to clean the mud off his cleats between holes too," Rocky offered sarcastically.

"No, I'll take care of that," Andy said, attempting with absurdity to defuse Rocky's mood. "But maybe you could pull the tab open on his can of beer when we make the turn. I can't risk having him cut himself doing it himself."

For a moment Rocky did not catch Andy's playfulness. "How deep are his pockets anyway?" Rocky said, impressed with Andy's deference toward a schoolmate who may have been envied but not respected years ago.

Andy answered soberly. "Deeper than ever. Dwight's become a helluva a business man." Andy stopped in mid thought as he saw a cart approaching from the club house with Dwight Kensington driving it. It stopped on the path behind the cart Andy had brought and the tall figure of Dwight Kensington stepped out and strode toward Rocky with a broad smile on his face. Rocky would have been pleased if Dwight Kensington had grown thick around the middle; however he still had the broad-shouldered, slim-waisted body that he had had as a collegian. Even in his youth he had never looked powerful because his chest did not have the depth to augment its breadth. However, he still walked with the litheness that gave a football coach the hope that he would be an extraordinary pass receiver.

At least six inches taller than Rocky's five feet nine, Kensington looked down on Rocky with a broad smile as he extended his hand. Rocky smiled ironically rather than from the pleasure of meeting his long-ago irritant. He noted that Kensington's face was not wrinkled nor his hair more sparse. His appearance underscored precisely what he was to Rocky, an affluent man whom life had apparently treated with kindness. Rocky, whose own success established that he need not be humble, would have been happier if Kensington showed some ill effects of life's buffets and pains rather than looking like he had not only mastered life's challenges but retained his youth and vigor in the bargain.

"Rocky, what a pleasant surprise to see you," said Kensington as he firmly gripped Rocky's tentatively extended hand.

"Dwight," Rocky responded tersely, then for fear of seeming unfriendly, added, "I've just been enjoying a look at this nice layout."

"It is well-designed, isn't it?" Kensington responded. "Truth is, it's a nicer course than the one I play during the winter in Florida, and it costs about ten times as much to belong to that one."

Rocky noted that Kensington's establishing financial pre-eminence had been gotten out of the way early. "So you spend the summers here near you childhood stamping grounds?" Rocky asked.

"Mostly." Kensington answered, "except for flying up to our place in Canada. Fishing's great up there, thank God," Kensington smiled. "Gives a guy some relief from playing golf."

"You don't enjoy the game?" Rocky frowned in surprise.

"Truth is," Andy injected, "his wife's the fanatic golfer in the family, right Dwight?"

"I can't argue with that, Andy," Kensington nodded. His pride was visible in telling Rocky, "She's won the women's championship flight club tournament here for the last three years running."

Rocky began to examine the rental clubs Andy had brought for him on the cart that he would be using alone. "Although I'd like to meet her, I'm glad she's not with you today. I suffer enough embarrassment with this game without having to play with club champions."

"Does Beatrice play, Rocky?" Kensington asked.

"Only rarely, Dwight, thank God. Those few times I coax her out, she makes it look too easy."

Andy, who had been swinging a pair of clubs as part of a loosening up ritual, said, "I think we're clear to hit now, Purple Raiders." He looked to see how his college contemporaries would respond to their team nickname of decades ago.

"You sure that it wasn't Black and Blue Raiders?" Rocky asked recollecting the less than glorious outcomes they had endured against several regularly stronger opponents.

Kensington went toward his bag of clubs and told Rocky, "If we're going by the higher number of yards per catch as a Purple Raider, you're up first, Rocky."

Rocky was pleased to find that his statistical besting of Kensington, which been a significant sore point when he lost his position to Dwight, no longer produced any irritation. He hefted the unfamiliar driver and responded, "But I'm guessing that if we're going by the highest handicap in the group, I'm hitting last."

Andy Turnbull, who guessed that Rocky's game had not miraculously blossomed in late life and knew Dwight's handicap, stepped to the tee confidently as the best golfer of the three. He asserted, "I'm not even going to try to out-humble you two," as he teed up his ball to begin play.

The threesome's game proceeded pleasantly enough for several holes. Maintaining the hitting order was not problematical. Andy's score on each hole easily fixed him with the honor of teeing off first. Rocky's and Dwight's indifferent hitting of a mixture of good and errant shots left them each good-humoredly claiming the dubious honor of hitting last. Rocky was surprised at Kensington's mild self-deprecation and began to join Rocky in backhanded complements of Andy for his superior play. When Andy announced his score on the fourth hole as his third consecutive par after a boggy on the first hole, Kensington said, "Damn it, Rocky, I should have warned you to count Andy's strokes, or we'll be hearing doubtful claims of par all day."

"How can it be my job?" Rocky countered with mock defensiveness. "I've been on the opposite side of the fairway from you guys every hole looking for my ball in the tall grass."

"Hell, at least you can putt the damn thing," Kensington sighed. "I took a gimme after four futile punches on that last green."

Rocky took a shortened practice swing and spread his arms palm upward in a gesture of basking. "Hey, it's a beautiful day and I'm not playing any worse than I usually do. The only irritation is Andy's good-naturedness. A low scorer who's so good humored and consoling about my bad shots is a real pain in the ass."

Kensington said he agreed with that, to which Turnbull offered to take delight in whatever troubles his two old friends got into if it would make the pair of them happier. Somehow Rocky enjoyed being bracketed with his old collegiate irritant as he and Kensington looked at one another conspiratorially in response to Turnbull's feigned irritation.

Off the next tee, Rocky and Dwight Kensington both hit their balls for good distance but into the rough on the right while Andy hit for good distance down the left side of the fairway. It was logical that the two former competitors, Kensington with several clubs on his lap, ride together in search of their errant shots while Andy rode directly to his ball in the fairway.

As they rode toward where the balls might likely be, Rocky asked, "So, Dwight, how familiar are you with that wild looking patch we're going to be looking into?"

"My wife says they ought to name if for me, since I spend so much time there."

"I take it she isn't familiar with the place herself."

"She's never hit a ball into there that I recall," Kensington said, smiling reflectively.

Rocky smiled, "I assume she plays often?"

"Three times a week, at least. She loves it," Kensington said. "I hope it's a coincidence that she agreed to marry me after she played this course the first time."

Rocky chuckled. "I'm sure that there were other reasons, even if that was one of them."

"Well, even if the golf course was what it took, I don't mind. I feel so glad to have her. I haven't had much luck in marriage. Sandy's my third wife, you know. It's a good thing she's got good values, because I'd give her anything she wanted whether it made sense or not. Between us, Andy's been tip-toeing around me to fund the club tournament. I'm letting him work up to asking, but Sandy'd be disappointed if I didn't, so I'll say yes when he finally gets around to asking."

Actually Rocky didn't know the specifics of Kensington's marital problems. Mindful of Andy Turnbull's request that he stay away from the subject of marriage, he wanted to change the subject. Fortunately, they had arrived at the approximate location of their tee shots. Rocky stopped the cart and said, "Damn, it's a jungle in there. I don't know about you, but it won't take me much of a look before I decide to drop a ball."

"I see that we use the same system," Kensington said as he turned in his seat on the cart and peered at the underbrush. "Well, Rocky, I forgot to put my machete in the bag. Tell you what," Kensington continued and reached into his pocket, "why don't I treat us to a couple new balls and leave those to for the people who enjoy exploring more than they do golf. In fact, take a few more with my company logo and try to lose them in the fairways around the west coast. It might help my business out that way."

"I did not realize that you had grown into a man of such wisdom, Mr. Kensington," Rocky laughed while pocketing the extra balls Dwight offered. Soon they had hit from the edge of the fairway and were riding amiably toward the green to join Andy, who stood on the edge of the green waiting for them so that he could putt.

At the end of nine holes, they stopped for a drink at the building situated near the ninth green to provide refreshment to players at the midpoint of their round. Dwight had just departed for the restroom when Andy asked Rocky if he were enjoying the round. Rocky responded that it had been very pleasant. He had hit just enough good shots mixed in with the bad to make the game pleasant irrespective of an abysmally high score.

"And how have you found the company?" Andy asked, in the light of Rocky's concern about being thrown together with his old competitor, toward whom Andy was aware that Rocky had never fully overcome his pique.

"Not a problem, Andy," Rocky answered as he raised the can to swallow the last or the beer he had been drinking.

"No sensitive stuff has come up, right?"

"Come on, Andy," Rocky retorted impatiently. "I'm not going to cause you a problem. Besides, Dwight doesn't seem to me like he needs to be babied."

Andy looked over his shoulder to see that Kensington was not returning. "You did know Dwight's first wife, Sheila, didn't you?"

"If I did, I don't recall."

"She came as a freshman when we were seniors, just as Dwight did. Cute little, well-stacked blonde. Dwight started dating her as soon as she got there. Theirs seemed like a match made in heaven. She made clear from the day she stepped on campus that she had no time for the typical Glassport State male. She measured the depth of Dwight's pockets early. You obviously don't remember when they walked into the Christmas dance. Dwight was the only guy wearing a tux and she had on a white brocade, bare-shouldered gown and a purple orchid corsage about the size of a catcher's mitt. And tanned? Winter in Pennsylvania and she looked she just returned from the tropics."

"I didn't do dances in those days, Andy. But if I'd been there with Treece I probably wouldn't have been able to take as close notice of Dwight Kensington's date as you apparently did."

"Recalling how modest the financial resources were of most Glassport State students in those days, you can imagine what an impression Dwight and Sheila made: that six foot three broad-shouldered, lean body of his in a perfectly fitting tux dancing with that cute, busty little doll that barely came up to his chest. They looked like royalty plunked down in the midst of a bunch of well-scrubbed, earnest peasants. And they continued to be noticed as an ideal couple for the rest of the school year. They married in June shortly after Ken graduated.' "

"I gather that they did not live happily ever after?" sighed Rocky in recognition of the obvious.

"Since the current Mrs. Kensington is number three," Andy nodded, "it is safe to say that your assumption is correct. Less than four years after they were married, Sheila left Dwight for a dumpy, middle-aged, divorced man who possibly was the surrogate father that Dwight had not managed to be to her or had not wanted to be. To add insult to Dwight's injury, she had been screwing the guy for at least a year before she left."

Rocky rubbed a frown off his forehead, "I hope you are at least going tell me that she fell in love so passionately that she left our rich, handsome college acquaintance for a penniless man."

"Please," Andy smirked, "what's the point of running to daddy if he can't buy you things? His pockets were even deeper than Dwight's, at least at that time."

"Dwight really loved her, huh?" Rocky asked.

"It seems the case, but about three years later he married a woman whose name I forget, and I'll bet Dwight wishes he could too. She looked like Sheila's twin in both appearance and attitude, and in less than a year the outcome of the marriage wasn't much different."

"So I conclude that it wasn't just in football that there were some low blows our friend Dwight Kensington couldn't handle," Rocky said. While shaking his head, he added, "That's some incredibly bad luck for a guy who was able to give two women whatever you'd assume they needed to be happy."

Andy jabbed a cautioning finger toward Rocky and countered, "Count your blessings, my friend. You managed to pick a real winner yourself."

"Yes," Rocky sighed contentedly, "Dwight's marital problems make coach Hixler's choosing him to spoil my last college football season pretty small stuff in comparison. I'm glad he seems to have come out of it all right."

"Of course, Hixler was not totally without his reasons. You have to agree Dwight had a lot more reach than you did," Andy smiled mischievously.

"Ah, bullshit," Rocky responded rather warmly about something of which the significance and the occurrence was decades past. Lowering his tone to normal, Rocky asked, "Did you invite me out here today just to piss me off."

"No, but I see that it is just as easy to do as it was years ago. Anyway, getting back to Dwight," Andy entered hastily, "he did hit it right with wife number three. Sandy Kensington is a gem, though she does look like Sheila caught in a time warp."

"Really?" Rocky gasped in astonishment.

"Oh, yes," Andy affirmed. "She must be twenty-five or thirty years younger than Dwight. She's one of those women who is always looking after her man without being clingy. Very athletic. Loves her golf and tennis. But the main thing is she dotes on her man. Seems to let him call the shots and is happy with that. Kensington is devoted to her. Her sports cars hardly has a chance to get dusty before Dwight gets her a new one. I don't know which the other wives at the club drool more over: her jewelry, her body or her knack for relating pleasantly to a room full of men while still making Dwight think he is the center of the universe."

Rocky surprised himself by being pleased that Dwight Kensington had found marital happiness. He smiled wryly, "I don't know how the poor man bears up."

"Somehow, he does. It must be the strength of character they instilled in us in college," Andy chuckled without a hint of seriousness. Then, noticing that Kensington was approaching the table, he devoted himself to the last few swallows of his beer so as not to delay their proceeding to play the back nine.

A few holes into the back nine, Rocky and Dwight were again riding together toward tee shots that lay on the opposite side of the fairway from Andy's. Kensington asked if Beatrice was well. When Rocky responded tersely that she was fine, Kensington confessed somewhat hesitantly that, for several years after he himself had finished college, he had envied Rocky his marriage. Rocky responded solely with a brief eye-to-eye contact with the man who had briefly dated the woman who later became Rocky's wife.

"I didn't have much luck with marriage myself for a long time," Kensington said. Fearing the beginning of a conversational topic Andy had asked him to avoid, Rocky was relieved to find that they had reached the two balls sitting near one another on the edge of the fairway in good position for a shot toward the green. Clearly more interested in telling his story than addressing his shot, Kensington proceeded to tell Rocky with great candor the story of his first and second marriages.

To avoid making any response, Rocky took his stance to hit his shot although his ball was a few feet forward of Kensington's. After his solidly hit shot flew down the fairway and bounced slightly to the right of the green, Rocky turned to Kensington and began penitently, "Oh, hell, Dwight, what's the matter with me. It was your turn to hit. I'm sorry, I guess that I was focused so much on my shot that I didn't notice that it was your honor."

Kensington laughed heartily. "Think nothing of it. I was so busy gabbing that I didn't even give a thought to addressing my ball. That happens a lot to me; especially when I have business on my mind. It drives my wife crazy. When she gets on the course, golf is the only thing on her mind. Sometimes I think she'll hit me with a club if I don't stop thinking about business and get my mind back on the game." Dwight Kensington was smiling absentmindedly. He obviously was recollecting with pleasure his wife's chastisement for letting business intrude on his recreation.

"You're pretty stuck on that woman, aren't you, Dwight?" Rocky grinned at his former sports adversary.

"I can't believe how lucky I am to have her, Rocky," Kensington answered seriously. "It must be that way for you with Treece, right?"

Rocky answered affirmatively immediately and then spent the rest of the round puzzling over whether or not his answer had been sincere or an automatic reaction. Had the readiness of his answer indicated a firmly held truth or was it a hasty response given without thought rather than from conviction?

After golfing, Rocky and Andy were still in the locker room after Dwight Kensington had gone ahead to the dining room after assuring them that he would have drinks ready for them as a prelude to their being his guests for lunch. "Well, Andy," Rocky began, "did you ask Dwight to bankroll the club tournament?"

"No," Andy nodded and sighed disappointedly. "The timing just didn't seem to be right. He's in a funny kind of mood today."

Rocky frowned. "He seemed in fairly good spirits to me."

"Oh, yeh, he's jovial enough, all right, but somehow he seems not his usual self. In fact, he must have mentioned several times while we were riding between shots how much he's enjoyed seeing you today."

"Really?" Rocky said and surprised himself by smiling. "It hasn't been bad, actually. All part of a very pleasant round, Andy. I'm glad you invited me."

Andy turned from the mirror where he was putting the final touches on his carefully combed hair, "You know, Rock, since you and Dwight are getting along so well today, maybe you should be the one to ask him to fund the club tournament."

Rocky looked up from tying his shoes and chuckled so heartily that his shoulders shook. "Andy, get control of yourself. I'm not even going to explain how ridiculous an idea that is."

"Hey, whatever works, pal," Andy reasoned. "You know me, always the pragmatist. Always go with the approach that will succeed."

"Well, that approach won't work."

Andy muttered, "I wish I knew what would."

Rocky knew from his dialogue with Kensington that Andy's success in getting Kensington's contribution was a certainty if he merely would ask, but chose not to tell him that. He decided instead to arrange for Dwight to get a little something extra for his money and give some added pleasure to the wife he obviously treasured so much.

"I'll tell you what might improve your chances, Andy." Andy sat down next to Rocky and looked attentive. "Ken tells me his wife had been the club's women's champion for three years running. That suggests to me she probably will win again this year. Why don't you suggest that it's time the club inaugurated new and more impressive trophies for the winners this year? I'll bet the thought of his wife getting something like that would prompt him to come through for whatever figure you need for the tournament and the new hardware."

Andy, who was an above-average golfer but one who had never risen to the level of a competitor for the club championship thought for a while with a glazed over expression on his face. Rocky concluded that Andy was thinking how he would feel if he had a realistic chance of taking home for a year a large, silver cup with his name engraved at the top of the plaque on the base which would carry the names of the successive winners for a number of years.

Emphasizing his idea with the motion of a golf swing, Rocky said, "I'll bet that if Dwight's wife were competing in the championship flight for a big new silver trophy, he'd give you plenty of bucks to underwrite the club tournament."

"That's probably true," Andy said thoughtfully. "maybe we could even improve the prizes for the non-championship flights and get the entire membership more interested in the tournament." Andy's brow furrowed in thought. "Maybe Dwight would go for the whole package."

Rocky smiled disingenuously "Well, pal, looks to me that it's up to you to sell the case for the money in a subtle way. You've got to plant the possibility that Dwight's wife might have a chance to bring home some classy hardware that she'll be proud to show off and make Dwight think that the idea occurred to him without prompting."

Andy face was locked in concentration for a short time. Then he said, "Why don't you go ahead and join Dwight for lunch. I'll be along in a few minutes."

"Take your time. I suspect Dwight's going to be happy to see you no matter when you get there."

Dwight Kensington and Rocky finished one beer and had begun another when Andy Trumbull, his face beaming with a broad grin, approached their table from the far side of the dining room. As he pulled out a chair to sit down, Rocky noticed he had some brochures in his hand. "What do you have there, Andy," Rocky asked, perfectly aware that the question was precisely what Andy hoped for.

"I just got some information I've waiting for."

"Really?" Rocky asked, continuing with his puppet's role.

"You might be interested in this, Dwight," Andy said. Rocky smiled in admiration of Andy's studied casualness. "I've been trying to convince the club officers that the time has come to purchase some new and more impressive trophies to award to the winners of the annual club tournament." He spread the colorful pictures of silver loving cups set on substantial, rich hardwood bases carrying large silver plates on which could be engraved the names of champions and the year of their success. Dwight studied the figures which disclosed the impressive size of the trophies. Dwight nodded, "Very nice. Will you have them for this year's tournament?"

"I don't know if we'll even be able to get them. We still are short of funding for the tournament itself, let alone any upgrade of the trophies," Andy said with a sigh of impressive soulfulness, Rocky thought.

"What do you need?" Dwight asked.

Andy mentioned a figure substantial enough to cause Rocky to raise his eyebrows.

Dwight matched Andy's offhandedness and said, "I can handle that for you," before he began searching the dining room for a waitress to take their lunch orders. "Man, we could starve before we get any food around here."

Andy immediately lost his nonchalance at Dwight's saying he would provide the funds he was hoping for. "Terrific, Dwight. You're going to be impressed with the entire weekend we're getting up for the event. And I'll see you get ample mention in the program."

"No, no , no," Dwight said, "don't do that."

"Why not," Andy asked.

Dwight smiled broadly. "I'm figuring to have one of those trophies in my house for the coming year, and I wouldn't want anyone to think I only helped out because I thought my wife was going to win, which I do, of course."

"There's no guarantee of that," Andy said with a note of concern in his voice.

"Of course," Dwight said, adding, "Ah, finally," as a waiter approached.

After they ordered their lunches, Dwight said, "Funding the tournament will probably be the least of my expenses connected with that event. Considering the substantial sum Andy had requested, Kensington's two companions stared at him with puzzled expressions. Responding to their dumbfounded expressions, Kensington explained, "You two don't know the drill, I see, no doubt having sensible wives. Sandy'll need several new outfits to wear in the tournament and some new jewelry, not gaudy but eye-catching. And who knows what else." Kensington looked as though he would be delighted at every dime that was spent."

"I'm glad she likes the layout," Rocky said, unaware that such was actually the case, "Or you'd be planting some tall specimens of her favorite trees here and there between the fairways."

"Oh, God, don't give her any ideas," said Dwight, pretending to be horrified while he looked like he might be contemplating checking with his wife about that.

Dwight raised his empty beer bottle to signal their waiter, who was now some distance away, to bring a round of drinks while they waited for lunch. When they sat with fresh bottles of beer in hand Andy raised his bottle toward Dwight and said, "Here's to you, my friend, you solved a very big problem for me,"

"What do you think, Rocky?" Dwight said, nodding in Andy's direction, "pretty expensive guy to be around."

"Yea," Rocky nodded, "but at least he's careful with money."

"Is he? But would you buy a used car from him?"

"Buy a used car from him?" Rocky mouthed with feigned grumpiness. "Didn't you notice that I checked to see if the golf balls he gave me to use had been fished out of a pond?"

Their energetically consumed meal was near its end when Rocky introduced the subject of the eulogy of Dave Christiansen that he was preparing for the next night's reunion. "I hope you make it a good one," said Andy Turnbull. "He was a helluva guy."

"That's for sure," seconded Dwight Kensington. "He saved me from a mountain of trouble."

Kensington's statement puzzled Rocky, who knew that Kensington's career in business had been distantly removed from the profession of education. Nor had Dwight lived anywhere near the school system in which Christiansen administered. It seemed impossible that Dave's professional activities would have impacted Kensington's life in any way. "How did Dave spare you some trouble, Dwight?" Rocky asked.

"Some time back, about twenty years ago, I'd guess, the governor was filling a spot on the Glassport State board of trustees. The two names under consideration were mine and Dave's. The president at that time--I forget his name; he didn't last long, as I recall -- was pushing for me. I've given some money to the baseball program fairly regularly, and I guess it was the president's way of showing his appreciation."

"Or to set you up to give more money," Andy said.

"He would know," Rocky said, nodding toward Andy.

Dwight smiled through the interruptions and continued. "The faculty union had proposed Dave for the opening. Logically, they figured that his record as an educator meant that he'd be a board member sympathetic to their interests. When Dave found out my name was under consideration, he called me and offered to withdraw his own name. I told him that I was only a candidate out of obligation rather than interest, and that I wished he'd keep his name under consideration. Well no one was happier than me when he was picked."

"So saving you the loss of you time was the trouble he saved you?" Andy asked, his frown revealing what little significance he placed on the outcome of the tale.

"No," Kensington responded with a vigorous shake of his head. "Something happened during Dave's term on the board that I thank heaven I was never involved with directly. In fact, the situation only turned out as well as it did because of Dave's efforts as a board member led to a solution that I never would have imagined or supported if I had been on the board."

The focused silence of his two listeners was all the request Kensington needed to offer the details related to his last statement. "About two years into Dave's term on the Glassport State board of trustees, the administration and the faculty union were at the point of having to negotiate a new contract. The administration had chosen that point to propose a major departure in the way faculty were paid."

"Let me guess," offered Andy Turnbull, whose career as a middle level manager in a building supply company had not made him a great admirer of employee unions, "they proposed that the faculty should have to actually work a forty hour week."

Rocky could not tell how seriously Andy held the cynical view he had expressed or whether he was posturing for the man whose money he wanted to be sure was delivered to underwrite the club golf tournament. "What was the big change, Dwight?" Rocky asked, smiling benignly at Andy.

"Instituting a merit pay plan," Dwight Kensington stated. "Up to that point, the faculty were paid according to a rigid salary scale that was based strictly on seniority and a promotion system was pretty much automatic during a person's length of service. The result was that effective teachers, boring drones, productive scholars and brain numb non-performers got exactly the same annual salaries. Whether for the right reasons or the wrong, President Ambridge and the board decided to change the pay system."

Suspecting what the answer might be, Rocky nevertheless asked, "What improper reason might there have been for such a change?"

"Of course the legitimate reason for the change, as we all know, is to stimulate incentive and pay the effective performers better than the drifters. However, the truth--even evident to a less than fully enlightened entrepreneur like myself--is that merit pay can also be a powerful tool for keeping employees under one's thumb, though there isn't an entrepreneur who's admitted that in two hundred years."

Andy Trumbull groaned as though struck and Rocky opened his mouth and gasped a mock expression of astonishment. "Andy, who is this guy? And what have you done with Dwight Kensington."

"Hey, screw you guys," Kensington retorted with no more seriousness than Rocky had conveyed. "My employees will tell you whether or not they're exploited, and I'm not exactly losing money. But guys like President Henry Ambridge, who are not even in a profit-making business, just want to use money to keep everyone in their place."

"And that's truly the wrong reason to want a merit pay system," said Rocky.

"Exactly," Kensington affirmed. "Anyway, the board didn't object to Ambridge's desire to put the merit pay plan on the table for the negotiations. However, it soon became Ambridge's frustration that the board had chosen Dave Christiansen to be their representative on the management negotiating team."

"Don't tell me Dave wouldn't support the merit pay plan?" Andy asked, his voice betraying disappointment.

"Come on," Kensington said. "You know Dave," Kensington responded as though their lifelong friend were still alive. "He was a manager. He knew the value of flexibility in pay scales. He also knew that Ambridge was a prick and that unions can overreach in their desires. Dave's the last guy in the world who'd buy a sack of bullshit from anyone."

"So how did it go?" Rocky asked with genuine curiosity.

"Ambridge thought the negotiations were going too slowly so he asked me to talk to Dave," Kensington reported.

"How'd he happen to choose you to do that?" Rocky asked.

"Ambridge would have said that it was only right to call on such a good friend of the university, Rocky," Trumbull interjected. "Not to mention wanting to encourage those contributions to the baseball program to keep coming."

Rocky smiled, "So he sent the deep-pockets donor and successful business man to talk to his old college buddy."

"Yes," said Kensington. "But, if Ambridge thought I would be cluing the sheltered educator on the realities of the marketplace, he couldn't have been more wrong." Kensington examined his empty coffee cup and looked around for a waitress.

"Well," Andy Trumbull said impatiently, "are you going to tell us about your meeting with Dave?"

Kensington looked at Rocky and nodded toward Andy. "Gets to be a pain in the ass after he gets the money out of someone doesn't he?" Kensington said with a smile.

"They never change," Rocky said, his unfairness covered by a jesting tone.

Andy snorted at the pair, "I had considered showing you two a little mercy on the course; now I'm glad I didn't."

"Better finish the story, Dwight," Rocky suggested. "His thin veneer of civility is rapidly disappearing."

Kensington spotted a waitress and raised his empty coffee cup when he had her eye. The coffee pot was soon on the way. "I set up a meeting with Dave and told him that Ambridge was hoping that he would use his influence with the union to convince them to support the merit pay plan. I told Dave that Ambridge felt his support was essential since the faculty felt that Dave was more sympathetic to their views than any other trustee.

"Dave told me that he favored merit pay but the time had not arrived for him to take a stand for two reasons. What the union was demanding as the quid pro quo for accepting the merit pay plan was not really the most desirable thing in their own interests. Besides, Ambridge would let the negotiations go to a deadlock before he agreed to the quid pro quo that they had proposed."

"Did Dave really know better than the union itself what was in the faculty's best interests?" Andy asked doubtfully. "Hey, the guy was the best, but he wasn't God."

"You know that for sure?" Rocky asked Andy playfully and said to Kensington. "What did the union want in exchange to accepting merit pay, Dwight?"

"Since the union had recognized that merit pay was inevitable, they felt that the participation of their members in the decision-making process would provide some degree of fairness. They wanted each faculty member's departmental colleagues to control the first step in the merit pay decision process by gathering the evidence of his performance and making the initial evaluation. The union proposed that the process, after administrative input, would be that a committee of faculty chosen campus-wide by the faculty would make the final recommendation to the president."

"Would that recommendation be binding?" Andy asked.

Dwight nodded negatively.

"So the final decision would still be in the hands of the administration," Rocky concluded.

Dwight nodded affirmatively.

"So the union felt that control of the process would guarantee fairness even though the administration isn't bound by the recommendation," Rocky concluded.

"Right. Of course there would another down side for the faculty," Dwight said. "Contesting the administration's rejection of a recommendation would be narrowly limited because the faculty had controlled so much of the process.

"Dave could see that, even if the union couldn't, that they had a better option to propose although they thought that their counter offer was the best they could hope for," Kensington said.

Rocky smiled thoughtfully. "So Dave had a better idea than they had themselves."

"Exactly," Dwight said with a wink. "When the deadlock had lasted what Dave considered the right amount of time, Dave told me, he was going to suggest to Ambridge that he make a major concession in order to get a merit pay plan. Specifically, he thought Ambridge should offer to let the reasoning behind the merit pay decisions be grievable. In exchange for the faculty agreeing to have the entire merit pay recommending process be in the hands of the various levels of the administration, the union would get a meaningful major concession."

"Weren't pay decisions already grievable in previous contracts?" Rocky wondered.

Dwight said, "Not the substance of the decision. An employee was not entitled to grieve the actual evaluation by the administration of the evidence for the decision; just the process by which the recommendation had been arrived at."

Andy nodded knowingly. "I'm sure that Ambridge loved the way things had been. As long as the rules were followed, the basis of the decision was incontestable. If that limitation were kept in a merit pay situation, he would have a lot more control than expanding grievability. Why would he go along with Dave's idea?"

"You found the sticking point, Andy," said Dwight. "However, Dave thought Ambridge would never get merit pay and limited grievability. And though he'd never say it to Ambridge, Dave thought that to have it both ways was more control than Ambridge ought to have. So, Dave told me I could tell Ambridge not to worry. He would support merit pay and insist to the union only that they needed to find a quid pro quo that was more acceptable to Ambridge."

Don't tell me," Andy grumbled, "that Dave went around the rest of the management negotiating team and planted the idea of expanded grievability?"

Dwight frowned at Andy. "You know better than that. Eventually, the idea of agreeing to merit pay in exchange for an expansion of the grounds of grievability occurred to the union negotiators."

"How convenient," Andy sighed skeptically.

"I'm sure these alternate ideas come up in the give-and-take of negotiations, Andy," Rocky said in a tone that cautioned that his admired friend had had the ethics to respect the maintenance of team loyalty in negotiations.

"Ambridge couldn't have been happy when the union dropped that idea on the table," Andy offered.

"His initial reaction was what you'd expect," Kensington said, "but at that point Dave helped him to see the advantages, and he eventually bought the deal."

"And the lion lay down with the lamb," Andy offered with exaggerated saccharin in his voice.

Despite your sarcasm, Andy," Dwight said, "I think that the university has been well served by the arrangement ever since." Andy, anxious not to distress the man who had just solved the country club's financial problem, assured Dwight that he had not meant to dispute that fact.

"A helluva guy, was our Dave," Rocky said. His two companions were vigorous in their agreement of his assessment. Rocky expressed his sense of obligation that the eulogy he was assigned to give the next evening at the reunion be worthy of their humane and benevolent friend. Dwight Kensington expressed his conviction that Rocky would do justice to his subject. In addition, Kensington said he looked forward to seeing Rocky again the next day. Rocky was surprised at the sincerity with which he himself said that the feeling was mutual. Andy was jovial as he drove Rocky back to rejoin Beatrice. Not only had he gotten the funding for the club tournament, but he was effusive about how amicably Rocky and Dwight Kensington had gotten along.

Chapter 9

That night, Rocky and Beatrice stayed at the most comfortable and pleasant hotel they had yet encountered on their trip. The attractive room and its amenities mellowed their mood. They were soon indulging in what had been a daily part of their lives in the days when they both had engaging careers. Rocky called it the daily report. Each related for the other's amusement or sympathetic response the activities of their day.

On completion of the daily report, a wider-ranging conversation inevitably ensued, permitting the Roccos to share their feelings and opinions on everything from the arts to politics, but most frequently on the latest doings and difficulties of their grown children, who were never far from their mother's consciousness and concern. Rocky often said that if one could not be born to wealthy parents, the next best thing was to be the child of Beatrice Rocco.

The final topic of today's dialogue illustrated the point. Beatrice's day with Martha Trumbull had been spent both sightseeing and shopping. Consequently Beatrice had purchased for the children additions to the annual gradual accumulation of clothes, gadgets and practical implements that would be part of the numerous packages that would be given them on their birthdays and at Christmas. Rocky's good natured banter at Beatrice for her additions to her cache of eventual presents was responded to with Beatrice's amiable verbal defense and gentle pats of her spouse as though attacking him to make him stop his remarks. Rocky wrestled his wife playfully to the bed and subdued her with kiss.

At its conclusion, Beatrice stood up. Rocky clung to her hand and said, "Remember when we were younger, staying in a hotel seemed to be some kind of aphrodisiac."

"I remember," Beatrice said with a softness in her voice that had been rare of late. "I concluded that it doesn't work for you any more, since we've been away from home almost a week and you haven't even touched me."

"I'm touching you now."

"Yes, you sure are," Beatrice murmured. She sat beside Rocky on the bed. Slowly, as though she were unsure of how Rocky would respond, she brought her lips to his. Years of distraction, conflicting obligations, inevitable annoyances and actual or imagined injuries faded for a time as Tony Rocco took wife into his arms. They proceeded to an intense interlude that was surprisingly satisfying.

Afterward, Rocky lay contentedly wondering if sex had ever felt better that it had during this unexpected interlude. Following that thought, what he took to be common sense intruded and dissolved the mellow mood that had been produced by their intimate activity. The pragmatic Anthony Rocco reminded himself that, where sex was the subject of one's thoughts, the latest experience always seemed to have been the best one. Nevertheless, he greatly appreciated the unexpected gift. He slipped out of bed, trying not to disturb the relaxed form of his dozing wife.

After quietly washing and dressing, Rocky drove to a nearby mall where there was a liquor store and a grocery. When he returned to the room, he was laden with champagne which was already cooling in a Styrofoam chest in which ice covered the bottle and more snack food than could reasonably be consumed by two sensible people. Beatrice was in a chair reading the notes Rocky had begun to organize into the eulogy of Dave Christiansen that he was scheduled to deliver tomorrow. Beatrice smiled at the sight of the food and drink he had brought. He could tell she was recalling that, in their younger days, indulging in wine and their favorite snacks regularly followed their on-the-road lovemaking.

As Rocky uncorked the champagne and poured two glasses full of the pale gold, sparkling liquid, Beatrice tugged open a bag of potato chips. Rocky handed her a glass of wine and Beatrice took it with a kittenish smile, "Am I being rewarded for being a good girl?"

"Define 'good'," Rocky countered with an exaggerated leer.

"I thought I demonstrated it rather clearly," Beatrice said with conviction.

"Very Effectively," Rocky responded agreeably, "maybe more effectively than ever." They drank, talked and ate with gusto. However, that did not deter them from going to dinner later, after which they took a short walk in the cool evening air. Then they returned to their room to watch television inattentively for a time before they settled down for a pleasant night's sleep.

The next morning, Rocky was shaved and dressed before Beatrice began to stir. As he often did when they traveled, Rocky went out to get some coffee and a paper to bring back to the room to permit Beatrice the leisurely start to her day that she preferred whenever the travel schedule permitted. When Rocky returned he found Beatrice awake and propped up in bed again reading the notes he had begun to organize for his eulogy of Dave Christiansen to be delivered that evening.

As Rocky set down a container of coffee and the morning paper on the night stand beside Beatrice, she gave a little shake to the sheets of paper in her hand. "This is very nice, Tony," she said. "I like your having focused on things that he did which show what a caring man he was. I hate those eulogies that are full of enormous generalizations and pious over-statement. Dave deserves better than that sort of speech. From the stories you've gathered, he seems to have been throughout his life the unusually humane, decent guy that he gave the potential of being when we knew him in college."

Rocky nodded in agreement. "That's just how he seems to have been to everyone I talked to except Tank. A pretty rare person, really. I was planning to put it in final shape while you read the paper."

Beatrice looked at Rocky with a bit of apprehension. "At the risk of suggesting a complication at this late date, may I make a suggestion?"

"What's that?" Rocky asked warily.

"You don't have any input from Carla. Don't you think that your eulogy ought to have some mention of his wife's feelings about the kind of husband he was?"

"They've always been a loving couple. You know that."

"We haven't see or talked to them for ten years, Tony. People do change."

"But Dave and Carla? I don't think so."

Beatrice smiled wryly, "Oh, you think that Dave is the exception in that respect too?"

"Well, Treece," Rocky admitted, "everyone changes. Sure. But a marriage is still a marriage. The bond is there always."

"And it's still the same?" Beatrice asked dubiously.

"Of course."

"Maybe you're just not paying attention," Beatrice said and returned to reading the morning paper.

Rocky began to study his notes. After shifting them about for several minutes, he put them down and looked at Beatrice. "Maybe there's something to what you say. Do you think we could stop and visit a while with Carla before we go to help set up the hall?"

Beatrice got up from her chair and said, "Then maybe we ought to have our breakfast and get on the road."

After all, we don't want to be late for the set-up-of-the-hall ritual, do we?" Rocky said with mock seriousness.

"Oh, heavens, no," Beatrice responded with a similar false tone of alarm.

The reunion was to be held, as in all previous instances, at a corporate lodge owned by the company for which one of the reunion participants worked. There was no cost to using the attractive and secluded facility. However, it was the task of the users to arrange the tables and chairs for the event, decorate the tables with whatever they preferred, in this case the Glassport State University purple and gold, and prepare the serving area for the caterer who was providing the dinner which would be served as an early evening meal. In this instance dinner would be served after the participants had spent several hours renewing acquaintances and retelling many old tales, grandly transformed from years of reiteration.

After breakfast at a restaurant near the motel, Rocky called Carla Christensen and asked if they could visit with her briefly to get some input for the eulogy Rocky was to deliver that evening. Carla was reluctant to visit with them, frankly admitting that she was still depressed over Dave's death although it was almost two years ago. Rocky persisted, pointing out that his eulogy would be missing an important ingredient if he were not to say anything about Dave as a husband and father. Carla reminded Rocky that he and Beatrice had often visited with them and surely had plenty of memories of the Christensens as a couple.

Rocky said that he had not forgotten that the periodic reunions of the group of Dave's college contemporaries had begun by invitation to the Christensens' home. Soon the gatherings outgrew Carla and Dave's home as the invitations extended to other acquaintances of the initial core group. Rocky said that Carla, who had not attended the same college as her husband, was nevertheless known to and liked by the sizeable group, who would want to see her at the reunion.

Carla hastened to make clear that she was not planning to attend the reunion because she wouldn't be able to handle the feelings it would produce. Rocky asked if she didn't think that her absence made it all the more important that her feelings of Dave as a husband and father be included in the eulogy. Carla capitulated to this argument and said she would actually be glad to see them if they would not expect that she would be anything like her old self.

The Roccos found that Carla Christensen was still the considerate and pleasant hostess she had always been even though her appearance showed the negative effects of her prolonged depression. After a brief period of uncomfortable small talk, Rocky felt he should get to the point for their visit before Carla wearied of their presence.

"Carla," Rocky began cautiously, "we don't want to intrude on your time too long. Let me suggest a way that we could minimize your having to dwelling on the loss of a man everyone in the reunion group loved and admired. I would like to tell you my perception of the relationship between you and Dave. If that is reasonably accurate to your own feelings, we need not continue to talk about things it is too soon for you to discuss."

"Let's try that," she responded with some relief.

"It seems to me that, in Dave, there was no difference between the public man and the private one. To friends and colleagues, he was truthful, accessible and loving. You and Dave seemed to me to have the most loving relationship of any couple of which I'm aware."

Carla smiled through her sadness and nodded, "I'd like to think it was. But, please, don't try to make it into something epic, because it wasn't."

Rocky was surprised at Carla's statement. He looked at Beatrice and saw that she seemed not to share his surprised feeling. At the risk of stepping into deeper water than he really wanted to, Rocky was about to ask Carla for elaboration of her statement when Carla spoke again.

"I don't know how love's been for you two. In fact, I've decided that none of us know what love is for anyone else. Maybe common sense begins when one draws the conclusion you'll never know what love is for anyone else and that that isn't important anyhow. For Dave and me, the passion cooled somewhere along the line. But the disappointment about that was very brief because something else remained—or maybe even got stronger."

Carla closed her eyes and continued, "My David was the kindest man in word and deed that I ever knew. And what amazed me and thrilled me all my life was that his unfailing kindness was not reserved to be spent beyond our home."

Carla smiled wryly and offered, "I know people like that, you know. They seem to have no kindness left for inside the home. It's all used up at work or in their solo social activities.

"I basked in the warmth of David's kind thoughts and actions all my life. It never stopped even when an unkind God gave him a lengthy and painful final illness. That's why I feel that no one can understand my loss."

Carla tilted her head as though to some people who were present near by, "Our kids don't understand They keep insisting it's time for me to be active again." Carla shook her head in rejection of the idea. "Maybe some day, but not yet. Maybe if I experience that feeling I used to have when David spoke to me or touched me in that kind, loving way."

Carla frowned, "Young people think that kindness is a poor substitute for love. If they're lucky enough to feel it some day, they'll understand." She looked at each of her guests and said, "It's that way for you two, right?"

Rocky and Beatrice both nodded in agreement. Rocky knew that he was not being truthful. He wondered if Beatrice was. Her face told him nothing. He focused on Carla and said, "Carla, I think we've intruded on your time long enough. I think we should be going." He stood and reached his hand toward Carla's. "We will miss you tonight. There will be a lot of people thinking about you and hoping that your grief will lighten real soon."

Rocky made a rather hasty exit while Beatrice hugged their hostess, and they exchanged some dialogue that Rocky did not catch. Back in the car, they road silently for some time. Rocky's thoughts were tied to what Carla had said. He wondered if Beatrice was focused on that as well. Finally he said, "Would you like to stop for some coffee before we go on to assist in the big set up?" Beatrice nodded her agreement and they both began to scrutinize the passing scene for a pleasant-looking possibility.

Chapter 10

It was early afternoon when the Roccos drove into the rolling green acreage of the corporate recreational property where the reunion would be held and proceeded toward the lodge. A half-dozen cars were already parked in the lot next to the stone and timber building. Their presence indicated that the preparation activity was already under way. As they entered the main hall, effusive greetings from the groups engaged in various preparatory tasks enveloped them. Beatrice headed toward a group of familiar faces working in the kitchen to prepare for the caterer, and Rocky walked across the main hall where tables and chairs were being brought from the storage room behind the massive stone fireplace that dominated the end of the room. The placement of tables and chairs to seat the eventual one hundred participants in the event had barely begun. Exchanging handshakes and shoulder pats with every male he passed, Rocky progressed to where his roommates of over four decades ago were loading eight foot long tables with folded legs out of the storage room onto a cart which would ease the movement of them to their locations around the main hall.

"You decrepit old men best be careful not to hurt yourselves," Rocky cautioned with sufficient volume to draw the two men's attention. Rocky's statement drew a whoop of salutation from the pair who were about to lift up a table.

Straightening up from his attempt to pick up one end of a table, Joe Dantine broadened the smile that seemed never to leave his face.

"Look, Marty," Dantine said to his fellow worker, "Tony Rocco misjudged the time and got here before we finished."

"Well, if he's as cheap as he used to be," Marty Pitarski responded, "he doesn't have a reliable watch."

"Will you listen to that?" Rocky said, raising his head toward the ceiling and exaggerating a gesture of astonishment. "Who's better at holding tight to a dollar than you, Pitarski?" Turning to Dantine, Rocky continued, "How many kids did he put through graduate school on a teacher's salary and still have a year's uncashed paychecks at home?"

"Three kids," answered Dantine, his voice carrying far enough that his co-worker inside the storage room would hear. "But he didn't have running water in the house until last year."

"Excuse me," came the sound of a chastising, shrill female voice from the other end of the hall, "could we have a little quiet so that we can rehearse here?" Rocky and his old college roommates turned and saw that the quartet of Glassport graduates who had sung together as collegians and were a staple part of the entertainment at these reunions were indeed assembled with sheets of music in their hands. Rocky recognized that the displeased speaker was Ronnie Barrett Summerfield, with whom he had met earlier in the week.

Joe Dantine chuckled "Your ass is in scalding hot water now, Rocky." Like the other Glassport collegians of long ago, Joe knew how seriously Ronnie took her singing. In fact she had performed professionally in summer theatre over the years, much to the delight of the husband now deceased who had been twenty years her senior. Unfortunately, his doting on her performances had nourished in her the illusion that her moderately good soprano voice was something much better than it was.

Thus, when she was to perform with her former college choral group for the contemporaries of her college years, she prepared and performed with perhaps even greater seriousness than when she had sung for paying audiences and the husband who invariably presented her with an armful of roses after her performances. She could not grasp that the reunion attendees were more interested in their conversations and banter while preparing the facility for dinner than providing ideal conditions for rehearsal. The other aged collegians were as engrossed in trading stories of their lives since college as Ronnie Barrett was in the rehearsal that she was engaged in at the same moment.

Toward the glaring Ronnie Barrett, Rocky made a gesture of feigned contrition as he whispered, "You better behave yourself, Dantine, or your wife will have to carry you home in a basket after Ronnie finishes with you."

"Me?" Dantine rasped in an outraged whisper. "You're the one with the booming voice. Remember what Dick Rosen said?" Dantine referred to a cherished mutual friend long since deceased. "Dick said that you were the only man who could play in a football game and broadcast it at the same time."

While Rocky snorted to suppress the sound of his amused recollection, Marty Pitarski approached Rocky and shook his roommate's hand vigorously, "Good to see you, Rocky."

"Be careful you don't bruise Pitarski's hand," said Dantine as he came to grasp Rocky's hand. "He doesn't need much of an excuse to get out of working."

As Rocky took Joe's hand he quickly surveyed the hall. "Three tables set up," he observed. "How long have you guys been working? Five, six hours? Maybe since dawn? It's a good thing I got here."

"Listen to that, Ski," Dantine said, nodding toward Rocky. His perpetual grin was the visible sign of a playfulness that had endured throughout Dantine's life from his collegiate years as an undersized but energetic football player noted as much for the relentlessness of his off-field pranks as much as his on-the-field enthusiasm. "You remember how much help he was last time, Marty? Just standing there bullshitting with one person after another while we did all the work."

"Hey," Pitarski began as he adopted an expression of elaborate condescension, "Pennsylvanians don't get many chances to see a California weirdo in the flesh. Naturally they want to hear if he can actually talk like a normal person."

Rocky studied Pitarski's lean frame that seemed not to have varied a pound from his college days. Undoubtedly a life of working as a public school librarian with a dedication bordering on compulsion had much to do with the preservation of Marty Pitarski's leanness. His devotion to enhancing the lives of his children had been not a burden but a natural expression of his serious nature. It was only around Joe Dantine that Marty could become playful. Thus it had been in college, and it was now still the case these many years later.

Rocky returned Marty's grasp and said, "Maybe you better get on the other end of those tables and we'll load up this carrier before anybody interrupts to talk to the Weirdo Outlander, Marty."

Rocky liked playing the weirdo from far away for the friends of his youth. What surprised him is the high percentage of them who had spent their lives close to their original home towns. Though an impressive number of them had had distinguished and lucrative careers, he felt that many of them had worked long and hard in jobs, particularly in public education, that had not absorbed the full use of the intellect and talent that they had. Perhaps he felt that way because he, on aged reflection, felt that his own career in the public sector had been a great waste of time.

With a touch of intellectual gymnastics, Rocky had escaped cynicism by reminding himself that he had freely chosen his path. He was more coldly objective in recognizing that the choice had only been possible because of Beatrice's sacrifice of her own interests. His conscience troubled him now to realize how long ago he had lost all consciousness of Beatrice's sacrifice to grant him his freedom.

Turning away from the task at hand, Joe said, "You guys go ahead. I'll be right back."

"Sure, Joe," Rocky said with disingenuous amiability, "just don't forget to be back for dinner at six."

Pitarski had already reached the back of the storage room and grumbled theatrically, "Hey, is anybody going to lift the other end of this thing?"

Rocky hastened to the task and by the time Dantine had returned there were four tables stacked on the wheeled carrier. When Pitarski had turned back into the storage room, Dantine nudged Rocky and motioned for him to observe as he bent down and wedged a folded piece of cardboard between one of the front wheels and the floor of the carrier, which would keep the wheel from turning. Pitarski yelled from within the storage room, "Hey, Tony Rocco, have you quit already?"

"No, no, Marty, be right there," answered Rocky and rushed to take one end of the table and assist Pitarski to set it atop the stack on the carrier. The carrier now being fully loaded, Joe leaned into the side the stack in position to push the carrier and directed, "O.K., Ski, give it a good shove."

In reality, Dantine only feigned applying effort to the load, so that when Pitarski shoved from the rear, the block against one of the front wheels that Dantine had placed caused the load to lurch in a quarter turn and send the stack of tables sliding off the carrier with a clatter that brought activity throughout the building to a stop. Everyone immediately saw that no one was injured and that there was nothing amiss except for five table tops spread like a hand of cards in an arc across the floor. The brief silence was followed by laughter in all quarters of the hall with the exception of where the rehearsing singers stood openmouthed. Rocky and his two co-workers found themselves the immediate target of goodhearted jibes about their physical weakness, ineptness and general lack of basic competence.

Joe Dantine stood with a broad smile and his hands raised in a posture that professed total innocence. Marty Pitarski eyed the carrier with a look of frustration that held it responsible for making him the focus of more attention than he desired.

Rocky had difficulty looking innocent since he knew the cause of the racket and had permitted Joe's prank to proceed. He believed that these gatherings, which had gone on for decades with great regularity, provided the participants with the pleasure of renewing acquaintance in a lighthearted atmosphere. Therefore, he did not feel apologetic for letting the incident proceed.

Of course, the sole exception to the general air of amusement was Ronnie Barrett Summerfield, who stood with flushed face and a badly tortured sheet of music in her hand. Her mouth moved rapidly as she directed a flood of words toward John Barth, the one person in their number who had worked diligently and tirelessly to replace Dave Christiansen in making all the arrangements for the reunion.

Soon John was headed toward the offending trio, who all struggled to adopt some appearance of contrition. John looked like an unenthusiastic messenger as he approached. "Hey, guys," Barth said with a pleading tone, "try to keep it down, O.K.? They're having trouble rehearsing the music for tonight's entertainment." Barth knew better than anyone else that the quartet would leave soon for the home of one of its members to relax and to dress in the outfits that they would wear to the reunion proper. Hence, he knew it was obvious to all that the rehearsal need not have been conducted at the reunion site but would have, with less complication, have been held where they would change clothes.

"It's these damn carriers, John," Joe Dantine said as he bent down and palmed the cardboard he had inserted by the wheel. "You know how the wheels jam sometimes." Rocky admired the air of innocence in Joe's performance. The genuinely embarrassed Marty Pitarski offered his apology and Rocky nodded to provide as much contriteness as he could offer without laughing. He suspected that everyone in the working party enjoyed Ronnie's annoyance as much as he did, since she had a long history of taking herself too seriously.

John Barth said pleadingly, "You guys know how seriously the quartet takes performing for the event. They need to rehearse to do their best." Rocky wanted to say that it was only Ronnie rather than the entire quartet who took the performance so seriously and that she should lighten up at this stage and circumstance of life. Instead, he joined his two old roommates in nodding affirmatively so that John Barth could feel he had mollified Ronnie and walk away relieved.

"You bastard, Dantine," Marty said when John was out of earshot, "I saw you pick up that cardboard just now. You used it to jam the wheel, didn't you, you prick." There was no heat in Marty's chastisement. He had decades of experience with Joe Dantine's pranks. Though he did not always enjoy the results when they discomforted him, he recognized that Joe's targets, occasionally including himself, often deserved their discomforture.

"Yeh, Joe," chimed in Rocky, "you should be ashamed of yourself." Rocky's chastisement dripped hypocrisy.

Joe's response rejected Rocky's insincere stricture with the insolence that it deserved. As the trio worked at restacking the five tables on the carrier, the amiable charges and rebuttals about who was at fault in causing the noisy interruption continued. Rocky was, as were his two old friends, engrossed in their enjoyable game of pseudo-blame. While other two managed to continue to whisper their retorts and allegations, Rocky's voice, as was his unconscious habit in the midst of an absorbing exchange, returned to what was for him a normal volume. Just as the last table was re-placed on the carrier, Rocky heard Beatrice whispering at his elbow.

"Rocky, they can hear you all over the room. Keep your voice down."

As quickly as she delivered her directive, Beatrice was gone, leaving Rocky with a feeling that had become all too familiar in recent years. He would perhaps tolerate his wife's chastisements better if he felt anger. What he did feel, and it always surprised him how deeply he did, was hurt and belittlement. His rational thoughts told him that her criticisms were most often warranted. Yet that understanding did not prevent his feeling like a child subjected to chastisement by an adult. Her strictures made him feel inadequate, like he was not an adult. Or perhaps it was that he felt that the adult that he was, and would continue to be, was unacceptable and unworthy. He saner moments told him that the devastation he felt was an overreaction. He realized that age had intensified an emotional make up that had always been hypersensitive.

He recognized that certain movie scenes of deep emotion that had formerly seemed merely effective drama now made his eyes well with tears. He knew that his body chemistry had changed with age. But none of his temperate realizations prevented the shriveling of his self-worth and confidence when Beatrice commented on some long ingrained element in his habitual behavior or lectured him on some detail of routine behavior of which he was as well versed and competent as she. His usual defense when he was feeling diminished and ego bruised was to withdraw. He chose not to say his feelings were hurt and would become taciturn and distant until the feeling of injury went away. Of course, he had recently planned a permanent withdrawn and would by now have made that escape if unexpected circumstances had not prevented his taking his little hoard of money and disappearing to start a new life--a peaceful existence for his few remaining years--safe from criticism for harmless, lifelong habits or inherent traits: the volume of his voice, the candor of his comments, the occasional omission of his established routines and the frequent unconventionality of his expressed thoughts. He recognized that he was imperfect from inborn traits or long held convictions; he thought he deserved to be accepted as he was without repeated correction, but he was denied this badly needed peace.

Rocky now concluded his escape plan had been overly concerned with needing a period of a few days before it was discovered. There was no reason that he could not disappear just as untraceably in the space of a few hours. The desire to do so was now newly awakened in his consciousness from the dormant place where the events of the last week had shrouded it. He resolved to be alert for his opportunity to grab his hoard and disappear as soon as he returned home.

With about an hour's further effort by the work party, the main hall of the lodge and the kitchen were fully prepared for the caterer and the larger group of Glassport State graduates and their spouses who would begin to arrive for the cocktail hour in the late afternoon. Joe Dantine regretted that they had no need to run the carpet sweeper to further disrupt the singing rehearsal. However, he was mollified when he noted that the group had already left for lunch, rendering the intended annoyance ineffective.

Beatrice had spent the time talking with several friends she had not seen for more than a decade, since their attendance at the succession of reunions had been sporadic. When she found that they were staying at the same motel as the Roccos, she suggested that her old friends go there with her and continue their catching up in more peaceful and comfortable surroundings.

Beatrice's plan prompted Rocky to tell her that he would drive to a nearby lounge with his former roommates and thereby not intrude on the tranquility and reminiscences of Beatrice and her friends. Unspoken was his desire for the greater comfort that he would feel to be avoiding Beatrice's company until he was feeling more sanguine toward her. With a sense of relief, Joe's and Marty's wives opted out of accompanying the three men certain that they were escaping more sports talk and exaggerated recollections of collegiate peccadilloes and triumphs, real and imagined, than they cared to endure.

In fact the old roommates' dialogue was as the absent wives expected until the subject turned to their recently deceased friend Dave Christiansen. After each had made clear his profound regard for Dave, Rocky said that he was concerned that his eulogy might not do justice to the man they so greatly respected and admired. He considered that perhaps he should let Dave's widow, Carla, examine what he had written when he had visited with her so that he could be assured that his tribute was appropriate and that he had not included any sentiment that Carla would find offensive. He said that he was surprised that Carla still seemed too fragile to come.

"We really coaxed her to come," Joe explained, "but she thought it would be too hard to be here with the entire group of Dave's college friends."

"Even after a year and a half that Dave's been gone?" Rocky asked.

"They were a very close couple, Rock," Marty said.

Joe nodded reflectively. "Close doesn't begin to describe it. They discussed everything--and I do mean everything."

"How would you know something like that, Joe?" Rocky asked with evident disbelief.

Joe studied the walls and ceiling of the dimly lit lounge as though searching to escape before he spoke. "Once I started bitching about Ruthie to Dave. You know how it is sometimes; you get to a point where you have to let it out--you know what I mean?" If the other two did not; they didn't say so. "Dave kept after me in that gentle but firm way of his until he pulled out of me one story after another of things that had happened or been said that had me so unhappy. After each one, he'd just nod and ask, 'did you talk to her about that?' After a while I'd said 'no' so often you'd have thought 'yes' wasn't in my vocabulary."

"Aw, no," groaned Rocky. "Don't tell me Dave gave you the old 'you've got to learn to express your feelings' speech? That's disappointing."

"He didn't lecture me on expressing my feelings at that point. He was a better teacher that that. Getting at the realities first was Dave's way. He just showed me that I wasn't talking to Ruth about anything that mattered. I told him that I couldn't bring myself to talk about some things."

"Is there a man alive who wants to talk about sex and money with his wife?" Marty said as he gazed at the residue of beer foam in his empty glass.

"There was one," Joe Dantine said. He looked at his friends with an expression both thoughtful and wistful. "You guys remember what Dave used to say so often in college that it was like a mantra for him?"

Simultaneously Rocky and Marty said, "Don't have contempt for the obvious."

"You got it," said Joe. "Dave asked me how anyone was supposed to know what is important to me or is distressing me if I didn't tell them. He suggested that I try saying the obvious. He said that's how he related to Carla and said that's how I could try relating to Ruth."

"Sounds too simple to be of much help," Rocky said, shaking his head decisively.

"See," said Joe to Marty as he gestured toward Rocky. "Contempt for the obvious. Too bad Dave's not around to straighten him out."

"I'll tell you what's obvious at the moment," Pitarski responded. "I need a shower and a change of clothes before we go back for the reunion, and I doubt very much if either of you smell any better than I do."

"That's it, Marty," Rocky said as he stood and picked up the check, "let us know exactly how you feel."

Marty smiled. "Don't be a wiseass or you'll be walking back to your motel."

In his room at the motel, Rocky spent more time after he showered and dressed than he would have anticipated thinking about Dave's advice to Joe Dantine while he waited for Beatrice to return to get ready for the reunion. It was Rocky's nature to be skeptical of truisms, especially those that were intended to be wise guides of human conduct. Perhaps the maxim that most drew his contempt was the maxim that most human conflicts could be resolved with good communication.

He thought of the many times it seemed obvious that disputants understood one another's statements perfectly but continued their dispute as vehemently as ever because neither one wanted to yield any minute particle of their original irreconcilable positions. In every really serious group conflict that he had ever been involved in, there was always someone who believed that all problems were soluble if people just 'made an effort to communicate.'

Never that Rocky could think of had that person actually been a significant contributor to a solution. It was always the person who was willing to give some ground who achieved the solution, but inevitably it was at the expense of some of his or his group's interests. Rocky recognized that such solutions were better than the pointless or even damaging continuation of a dispute. But it was the giving up, not the so-called communication which had been the key. There are times, Rocky reminded himself, when you just don't want to give up any more than you already had. You've reached your bottom line and the dispute continues until one party or another yields on some part of their position to that point. Until that time, there is no reason for talking.

He thought about his secret cache of twenty thousand dollars. He was at his bottom line; he felt that he was steeled for what he must do. For a few more days, he would be pliant and pleasant, then he would strike out for freedom.

Chapter 11

Walking into a reunion of his Glassport State contemporaries was always an emotional lift to Rocky. He could not explain why he felt so warmly toward these people, many of whom he did not know all that well in college and all of whom he had seen only rarely since then. However, he was invariably delighted to greet them and begin renewing acquaintance. He liked to hear the answers to his questions about their professional accomplishments. Their successes did not surprise him. His responses to their own queries about his life were rarely serious. He suspected that his old acquaintances secretly were surprised that he was not jailed or dead by misadventure since he had in his youth done as Mark Twain said of himself: that he had studied for the gallows. There were times when he pondered with some seriousness that he might had completed that curriculum had it not been for Beatrice's sobering influence. Rocky felt small when he thought now that he no longer appreciated her influence. He rationalized that there had been a change in the spirit of her guidance. Her suggestions seemed to assume he had learned nothing. They often seemed accusatory, or they gave him little credit for competence.

He put the well-worn complaint from his mind as he was approached by a familiar face wreathed in broad smile. Eddie Parsons carried a bottle of beer in each hand. "Rocky, you're going to die of thirst," Parsons said as he handed the one in his right hand to Rocky. Rocky, though not a frequent beer drinker, took the bottle with his left hand and reached to grip Eddie's hand with his right.

"I doubt anyone ever died of thirst around you, Eddie," Rocky offered. "However," he said as he raised the bottle toward his lips, "I'm not going to buy any insurance even if you feed me a case of this stuff."

"You'd have to talk to my son about insurance anyway, Rocky. I gave it up two years ago. Besides, I'm making more money playing golf against this patsy," Eddie said and nodded toward the man who was trailing a few steps behind him. "You remember Morton Harp?"

The man who now stood at Eddie Parsons's elbow smiled tentatively. "Hello, Rocky," he offered, his pale complexion emphasizing the hesitance in his voice. He had a white plastic drawstring bag in his right hand and a can of beer in his left. He let the bag drop softly the floor and extended his hand toward Rocky.

Laboring to recollect any memory of the man, Rocky gripped the extended hand and studied the man's face intently. Before the handshake become overly long, Rocky said, "We lived on the same floor of the same dorm, right?" Morton Harp nodded encouragingly but offered no other assistance. "Oh, hell," Rocky chuckled as he recollected the man. "It's Mort the Mighty." He turned to Eddie, "I used to call him that when I washed dishes in the university dining hall and he waited tables. No one else stacked so many dishes on a tray when he or she was clearing tables as this guy did. I always expected him to lose them sometime, but he never did." Rocky shook Harp's hand vigorously. "It's good to see you, Mort."

"Good to see you too, Rocky," Harp responded. "You've come a long way to attend the reunion." Rocky began to explain the special reason that had mandated his attendance when a woman strode up behind Harp and called his name.

Harp turned to an attractive woman whose carefully waved hair of silver mixed with pale blond strands and a smooth rounded face with rosy complexion made for a still youthful appearance. She was not slender but a well-cut powder blue suit made her buxom shape still retain some appeal. "Oh, Sharon," Harp said as though recollecting his duty. Prompted by the look of consternation on the woman's face, Harp seemed to need to explain himself, "I've just been talking to the guys."

Ignoring the presence of Rocky and Eddie Parsons, the woman said, "You forgot to put my other shoes in the car."

"No I didn't," Harp responded.

"I just went out to get them, They're not there," said the woman.

Harp bent down and picked up the plastic bag that lay near his feet. "I have them right here," he said, offering the bag to his wife. "I figured that by now you'd have had all of the heels you could stand for the day."

Sharon took the bag. "Thank you," she said coolly and turned toward some nearby chairs where she could sit to change shoes.

The trio of men watched silently until Sharon Harp had finished changing shoes. She dropped the bag which now contained her heels against the wall beside the chair and began to walk back toward one of the groups dispersed around the hall engaged in conversation.

"Another crisis averted," Rocky said amiably to Morton Harp.

Harp's pale complexion had a slight flush, and he answered with some resignation in his voice. "At least for the moment."

Rocky nodded sympathetically. "It's nice not to be found guilty, hey, Mort?"

"Actually, I'd prefer not to be accused," said Harp.

"What?" Eddie Parsons asked, "Don't you ever forget anything?"

"Of course," Harp answered, "but it would be nice not to have the assumption made every time that I'm at fault."

Rocky nodded his agreement. "You mean that you'd occasionally like to hear 'I can't find my shoes' instead of 'You forgot my shoes.'"

"Exactly," said Harp, punctuating his concurrence by pointing his finger toward Rocky.

Eddie Parsons laughed, "Well, aren't you guys the sensitive ones."

"Maybe your wife doesn't always assume that you've screwed up," Harp said.

"I must actually listen some time to notice if she does," Parsons said deflecting a possibly sensitive subject.

"I know how you feel, Mort," sympathized Rocky. "Maybe it's bothersome because she'd probably never be accusatory with anyone else but you."

"She's the soul of sensitivity with anyone else," Harp said.

"You guys are hypersensitive," Eddie maintained.

Rocky conceded, "I can't speak for Mort, but You're right about me. I'm different that way than I used to be. Years ago I'd have gotten angry and said something; now I just feel wounded and sulk. The accusation makes me feel diminished, like a kid being reminded of his labored-over failings, or being lectured about the obvious and familiar."

Harp mused, "Maybe wives change too. The person who ought to care most about a guy's feelings isn't any longer as sensitive with him as she is with others."

"Boys, boys," Parsons chided, "you're talking about 'feelings.' It makes you sound like a couple of a ladies at their sewing circle. Have you ever thought of just telling them to stop?" Rocky and Mort Harp looked at each other for some sign of affirmative admission. Their silence told Parsons all he wanted to know. "So they are supposed to read your minds about what's bothering you? Simplicity, boys, simplicity. 'Don't underestimate the obvious,' as someone once said to me."

"Who was that, Eddie?" Rocky asked, pretending that he did not know Eddie's likely source.

"Damned if I know. It was so long ago that I can't remember."

Mort Harp gestured toward Eddie. "He had to get it from someone, Rocky. It makes too much sense for him to have thought of it himself." Harp paused and shook his head slowly. "Funny, isn't it? You would think that the longer you live with someone, the easier it would be to talk to them, but it seems that it's just the opposite."

"So it seems," Rocky mused, thinking of how often he chose silence over candor in his relationship with Beatrice.

"Ladies, ladies," Eddie Parsons chided sarcastically, "let's go get another beer before I break down and cry over the sadness of it all."

Rocky and Mort smiled sheepishly and moved to follow Eddie's suggestion.

"And Mort," Eddie added, unable to resist a final jab, inaccurate though it was, "don't forget the damn shoes next time O.K."

Rocky smiled at the back of the rapidly moving Eddie Parsons, whom he had always considered the least likely source of wisdom in the nation and perhaps beyond. He said to no one but himself, "What it comes down to is that, if you want kindness, you better ask for it, and you better freely give as much of it as you'd like for yourself."

Chapter 12

The reunion meal began with little hope of calm and efficiency. In the interest of economy in paying the caterer, the planners had agreed to have the food be served through a buffet line. The choices of food were varied and abundant but within the familiar form of what passed for Italian food in Western Pennsylvania. (Actually stuffed cabbage, locally called pigs-in-the-blanket, perogies and pasties had intruded into the menu so as not to be a slave to the purity of one nation's dishes and to recognize that the mixed ethnicity of the region had resulted in a range of ethnicities being fond of one another's signature dishes.) The buffet line conversations were complicated and time consuming because couples and friends wanted to move through the line together and share a table, hence the process was turbulent but managed in good humor. Rocky found the menu a treat. As a native of the region who had eaten it varied ethnic fare with voracious appetite during his youth, he indulged plentifully in everything from spaghetti through pigs-in-the-blanket. Since choices also included the prime rib and mashed potatoes of Beatrice's upbringing, she was able to forego the unfamiliar ethnic choices and brought to the table as full a plate as Rocky.

After the noisy and lengthy meal, the program got under way with no greater efficiency than the meal, since the boisterousness that manifested itself in these periodic gatherings of lifelong friends had been intensified by a plentiful consumption of wine and beer.

The program began with the awarding of door prizes followed by the inaccurate singing of college songs that had never really been learned, all of which tended to increase the din and disorganization rather than quell it. However, a subdued air settled over the group when the master of ceremonies, John Barth, announced that Anthony Rocco would deliver a eulogy to their recently departed friend and the initiator of the reunions they had enjoyed over the many years.

Rocky took with him to the podium the stack of cards on which he had made his notes about the instances over the course of decades in which Dave Christiansen had constructively touched the lives of many of the people that he had known since his collegiate days. In addition, he had his notes about Dave's long and distinguished career as an educator. Rocky placed his notes strategically in several related stacks on the podium.

He looked at the expectant audience of familiar faces, then fussed again with his notes. Rocky was finding it hard to begin. Such difficulty was not a frequent experience for him. In fact, when he was at ease with his subject and was well-armed with material, public speaking was not only easy for him but an experience he relished. His reticence, he now realized, was his continuing fear that his eulogy would not do justice to the man they all had known and admired. He had planned to pay tribute to Dave by relating the constructive and humane benefits he had provided to many who were part of the audience seated before him. The problem was not a paucity of commendable actions to relate. The reverse was true. To relate them all would constitute a lengthy and rather typical eulogy.

The greater worth of their friend, Rocky concluded, was likely to get lost in the long presentation. Maybe it was irrational, but Rocky decided that a shorter eulogy rather than a recitation of the abundant material he had compiled would do more justice to their admirable friend if he managed to capture a single, appropriate theme. Aware that tension was building in the room as he had stood before the audience so long without beginning, Rocky began speaking more in desperation rather than decisiveness. He could only hope that what developed as he spoke would do justice to their revered friend.

"Many of you know that I have spent this week learning of the many things that Dave did to benefit those of us who were in difficulty of which he somehow was aware. The remarkable thing is that I did not have a single person say to me 'I asked Dave to help me.' Apparently that was unnecessary. If he recognized the need for help, he proceeded to help, whether the need could be best served in conventional or unconventional fashion. He needed no request or prompting.

"Dave Christiansen was a man who saw his way in life more clearly than anyone else I ever knew. What makes that clarity even more remarkable is that it was neither simplistic or selfish. He made it his task to affect constructively the life of any person who he recognized needed it. Often he helped so unobtrusively that the beneficiary sometimes learned of it after the problem was alleviated..

"I can assure you that there are people here who are unaware what he did on their behalf. There was a special wisdom in that. He could occasionally be an avenger as well as a benefactor. He was not only the most benevolent person I have heard tell of, but the wisest and most just.

"His professional accomplishments are familiar enough to you all that I need not mention them. Even those of us who did not work with him directly know of his service to education because of the recognition that was given it by our alma mater years ago. Yet I submit to you that his professional accomplishments pale in significance compared with his unselfish devotion to the best interests of the people he was able to help at critical times in their lives. Though I have not met with you all in preparing to deliver this tribute, I am convinced that there is hardly a person here who could not relate some instance when Dave's assistance helped resolve a crisis in their lives in beneficial fashion. I am amazed that it was always clear to him what he should do.

"That clarity of purpose is more complex than the plain recognition of it indicates. If Dave had been a selfish man rather than an unselfish one, he would have been monstrous. However, he was totally unselfish. My personal experiences have made me conclude that it is unremarkable that some people are astonishingly bad. What is remarkable is that some people are so amazingly good. Among those, Dave Christiansen was to me the most amazing of all. I was privileged to know him; I wish I had been more like him. I hope that you feel that way too."

Rocky stood silently at the podium as a heavy silence descended on the room and held the audience in its grasp. Rocky had not known what reaction to expect from his listeners, who were, like himself, Dave Christiansen's lifelong friends. The silence rested heavily on Rocky's shoulders as he stood at the podium a few moments longer. Then he started toward his seat. A feeling of embarrassment began to well up in him, and he was convinced that he had mistaken his task and its affect on his audience. He was devastated to have failed his friend. The silence meant that the audience had found the eulogy inadequate. In his desire to deliver an appropriate tribute to his friend, he had achieved exactly the reverse. Even Beatrice's reassuring squeeze of his hand could not dispel his embarrassment.

Rocky endured the rest of the program in discomfort, hoping to escape from the hall as soon as it ended. But as soon as the program ended with the best wishes of the master of ceremonies to all for a safe trip home, Beatrice rose from her chair at Rocky's side. She patted him on the shoulder and said she would soon return. Her absence added to his feeling of discomfort and added impatience to his desire to escape. He responded distractedly to the several people who stopped by to commend him for his eulogy. He was sure it was out of kindness rather than conviction.

Finally, Beatrice returned. Rocky began to rise from his chair so they could make a quick exit, but Beatrice asked him to remain seated so that she might talk to him about something. Rocky was surprised by the gravity in Beatrice's bearing as she looked at him.

"You know that there's a staff member of the university foundation here?"

"I remember," Rocky responded wryly, "even though his remarks of greeting on behalf of the university did not rise above standard fare so as to merit recollection."

"You have enough experience with similar assignments that you ought to be more charitable," Beatrice said. Then she smiled and added, "You always assume that everyone ought to match your standard of performance at the things you do well."

"Obviously you are being kind about today's fiasco in speaking of my performance standard," Rocky murmured morosely.

"No, you've often at your best when you feel you've done poorly. I can't have been married to you for over forty years and not know how you're never satisfied with yourself, or anyone else for that matter."

"Not true," Rocky responded emphatically. "Of course," he began with a crooked smile, "I'm almost always satisfied with you, though I'll admit that you have practically no company in that category." Rocky paused. His brow furrowed, "I suppose it's been years since I ever said I was pleased with you."

"Oh, well, you don't ever say when you're displeased either," Beatrice said gently. "If you didn't go a million miles away at times, I'd never know you're displeased, though I usually can't figure out about what. We've got to talk about that soon, but I want to talk about something else now."

Rocky was relieved at the change of subject. The setting was the wrong one for a subject so sensitive. "What's wrong?"

"Nothing's wrong exactly," Beatrice sighed, "but disappointing nevertheless." She squeezed her husband's hand and said, "I was so taken with what you said about Dave that it occurred to me that it would be a nice gesture to offer a scholarship at the college in his name."

"That is a good idea; a very good idea," said Rocky.

Beatrice said, "Well, since we haven't made any decision about our annual charity contribution yet, I asked the man from the foundation if it could be done with that amount."

"That's great, Teece," Rocky said, "I wish I'd thought of it myself."

"If you had, you'd only be as disappointed as I am," Beatrice sighed. "Our paltry five thousand isn't anywhere near the minimum needed to establish a scholarship endowment."

"What's the minimum?"

"Twenty-five thousand," Beatrice murmured. "Know where we can get twenty thousand?"

Rocky wasn't sure if Beatrice was serious, but the question nevertheless provoked thought. In fact, he knew where that exact amount was available. In his mind's eye he could see the twenty thousand dollars of cash--his freedom fund, as he thought of it--

that lay in the bottom compartment of his suitcase in the garage at home.

"As it happens, I do know where we can get twenty thousand dollars if you are serious about our contributing enough to establish a scholarship endowment," said Rocky.

Beatrice smiled, "I am serious, I think. Hearing your eulogy brought home to me how much I did admire Dave, and your eulogy makes obvious how much you respected him. If you'd like to have him remembered with a scholarship in his name, I'm all for it. Where do you think we can find the money?"

"Well, there's that small. paid up life insurance policy with a cash value of twenty thousand. Remember? It's the first policy we took out after we married," Rocky said. "We've got other assets, not to mention other insurance, that sufficiently cover your expenses and needs if I go first. We could just cash in that policy. After all, it's really your money. Added to our annual five thousand planned giving we'd have enough to establish the scholarship. Of course, we'd have to skip giving to some of the other organizations we usually support, but this is a special thing to be doing in Dave's memory."

"Were you as taken as I was by what Carla said about their relationship?" Beatrice asked.

"Very much," nodded Rocky thoughtfully.

"Perhaps the scholarship should carry both their names," Beatrice said. "And altruism aside, Tony, a contribution that size has very beneficial tax implications."

"That too," Rocky managed to say as he laughed heartily. Beatrice could never really suppress her practicality for very long. Rocky not only enjoyed the pecuniary results of Beatrice's interest in investment and budgeting, he derived pleasure from watching her engrossment in the pursuit.

"So we'll do it then?" Beatrice asked looking to confirm the commitment in both their minds.

Rocky nodded affirmatively. "Why don't you get with the man from the college foundation and tell him that we're making the commitment. When we get home, you can leave everything to me. I'll take care of cashing in the policy and getting a certified check for the full amount. You find out how it should be made out."

"I'd like to tell him that we want the gift to be anonymous, O.K.?" Beatrice asked.

"Fine by me," Rocky answered. He was a little surprised how easily he was surrendering his freedom fund. On the other hand, he was foregoing an action that would have surprised and puzzled Beatrice, their grown children and many of their friends. He would have to solve his problem in another way, Rocky concluded. He hoped he was not merely postponing the solution for which he had acquired his freedom fund, which in similar size might be impossible to arrange again. Of course, if he were serious about adopting Dave Christiansen as a role model, he might not need a freedom fund, now or never.

Chapter 13

It was nearly midnight of the following day when Rocky and Beatrice arrived home from their trip to the reunion. They stood on the sidewalk in the midst of their luggage while Rocky searched among his keys for the one to the front door. His only light came from the street light across the street and some fifty feet away. Beatrice looked at the totally dark structure and said to Rocky, "You forgot to put the lamps on the timer again." She was referring to their practice of putting several lamps in the house on timers that would light the house for the evening hours before a normal bedtime. There should have been some light showing through the closed drapes of the living room window and several other rooms if all was functioning properly.

"I'm sure I set the timers before we left," Rocky said.

"Then there ought to be a few lights on until twelve thirty. Or, if you did plug in the timers, you got the setting wrong," Beatrice reasoned.

Rocky was well past the point in life of claiming freedom from omissions and errors in performing life's little responsibilities. It fact, it seemed to him that his most frequent response to queries about having done some chore was that he wasn't certain that he had. But with advancing age, his conviction about the futility of dialogue had increased, so he did not re-assert his recollection of having set the timers before they left on the trip.

Unfortunately, he once again could not join tranquility to his silence. Hence, his injured feelings caused an uncomfortable crowd in the bed he settled into with Beatrice. After two hours of fitful sleeplessness, he got up to read in the hopes it might make him drowsy. Preparing to settle into his favorite reading chair, he unplugged the nearest lamp to the chair from the timer and plugged it directly into the outlet to give him better light to read by. It failed to light.

With a twinge of uneasiness, he reached for the switch on the lamp. If the light came on with a different setting of its switch, he had not put the switch in the on position before plugging the lamp into the timer, hence explaining its failure to light. He found that none of the lamp switch settings resulted in light. The bulb's having burned out rather than his failure to make appropriate preparations was the cause of the lamp's being dark when they returned home.

After fuming for a moment over Beatrice 's accusation of his having failed at performing a minor responsibility, Rocky fumed with double the intensity because he let himself be bothered by such a minor matter as her accusation. His consciousness of his pettiness did not diminish his agitation. Adding to his discomfort were his thoughts of the stash of cash in the garage and his foolishness in having committed it to something other than his escape. He knew that he could not change his mind because part of his plan to disappear included the presence of circumstances that would give him several days of traveling before his having gone would be discovered.

That element of having several days before his departure was noticed wasn't essential, he reasoned. He could walk out of the house in the morning with the money concealed in his clothes and be gone from the area, even though his having done so would be discovered in a few hours.

Strangely enough, that complicating thought brought sleep where lecturing himself not to be petty had not. He slept a bit later than he usually did, but it was only a few minutes after eight when he was awakened by the ringing of the bedside phone. Beatrice was not in bed. Rocky concluded she would have answered elsewhere in the house if she had heard the ringing. Before mumbling a sleepy hello, Rocky decided that Beatrice was in the garage doing the laundry that they had brought back from the trip.

Responding to his inarticulate greeting came the sound of the voice he found most pleasing in the entire world. "Grampa, grampa, is that you?" came the silvery sound of his five year old granddaughter Becca's voice. He detected from a quavering quality to the sound that all was not well with her at the moment.

"Hey, Becca, it's grampa O.K.," Rocky answered, trying to put a smile in his voice. "How are you, honey?"

"Mommy's being not nice to me," Becca stated, her voice sounding injured and close to tears.

"She's not?" Rocky responded with a sympathetic tone, though the possibility that Catherine, the Roccos' daughter, had been unkind to her child was one of the least likely possibilities imaginable. However, Rocky was certain, her unhappiness no doubt had some basis. Rocky thought of Becca as the oldest five year old in the world. She was very verbal and possessed of a degree of insight that both amused and surprised everyone around her. One was never sure whether her concise, candid assessments of people and events were happy accidents or precocious understanding, but it was delightful to hear her take accurate measure of an event.

"What happened, Becca?" Rocky asked.

"I picked mama a bouquet of the very prettiest flowers in the garden, big yellow and purple ones almost as big as my head, and she scolded me."

Rocky was glad that his granddaughter could not see his smile. "Why would she scold you for that, honey?" he asked, though he thought he knew.

"She said that I should have asked her first, but how could I surprise her if I asked first?"

"I guess she had some plans of her own for those flowers," Rocky said with a sympathetic sigh.

"She said that she was saving them for her meeting on Friday," said the contrite little voice.

"I thought it might be something like that," Rocky said.

"I thought she'd be happy. Besides, sometimes the flowers just stay in the garden until the petals fall. I don't like to be scolded when I meant to be good."

"Nobody does, Becca," Rocky offered with all the honey he could muster in his tone. "But don't feel bad. I'll bet your mom's already sorry she scolded you."

"I don't care if she is," asserted Becca, abandoning the meek tone that she only rarely used. "She hurt my feelings."

"Well, You've made me understand that, and I think you should tell her that too," Rocky suggested, responding with the proper righteousness to support the little charmer.

"She'll just say I'm stubborn."

"I'll tell you what. You tell your mom that grampa said she should remember that little girls have baby feelings," Rocky advised.

"That's silly, grampa. I'm not a baby. I don't have baby feelings." Rocky had no trouble discerning Becca's impatience.

"Becca, 'baby feelings' means soft, tender feelings," Rocky hastened to explain. "That's what your mom used to call how she felt when she was a little girl and I scolded her when she shouldn't have been. The truth is, everyone has baby feelings at times when they feel unfairly treated. You tell your mom that I told you to remind her about people having baby feelings."

There was the silence of uncertainty as Rocky waited. "Go on; you go tell her. Just put the phone down. I'll wait until you get back. I want to know what your mom said." Rocky heard the sound of the phone being laid down and renewed his smile as he waited.

He waited patiently, imagining the dialogue that was occurring between mother and daughter. It was no doubt a contest of equals despite the parental relationship. This was no more than Catherine should expect, since Rebecca was precisely as thoughtful and assertive as Catherine herself had been at age five.

It was the melodious voice of Rocky's daughter that came through the phone when it was picked up. Her amused wryness was evident as she said, "So, you've been undermining my authority with my child again."

"What would you know about authority, since you never recognized any from the time you were born?" Rocky said without gravity.

"You're never going to forget the 'baby feelings' thing, are you?" asked Catherine.

"Why would I? Until you created the term, I never realized that everyone one, including me, has baby feelings. You were so wise though so young, like Becca, who, like yourself, is a lover of flowers, I understand."

"It's possible for a child to have too much initiative, I think," offered Catherine.

"I won't hear of it. My granddaughter is perfect. Besides, the day will come when you will hope for her arrival bearing flowers for her mother."

"I suppose that's true," sighed Catherine. "How was your trip?"

"Fine," Rocky put in perhaps too hastily.

"How's mom?" asked Catherine.

"Hang on," said Rocky. "I'll get her and you can ask her yourself."

Rocky had shaved, dressed and was well into a bowl of breakfast cereal before the conversation between mother and daughter ended.

Beatrice sat down opposite Rocky at the dining room table and said, "You and Becca have baby feelings, I hear."

Rocky smiled and said, "Remember when Catherine said that?"

"Yes," Beatrice nodded. "I can't remember what you'd done to prompt her cautioning you, but she did it in her ever reasonable way."

"A born psychologist," Rocky grinned as he reminisced. "Never had a tantrum that I can remember, but always able to explain her feelings."

"Her father was not a very hard sell for her," Beatrice said with a mother's objectivity, recollecting a bright and charming child that occasionally needed to have a limit set for her.

"It's a wonderful attribute that Catherine has always had, being able to communicate one's feelings without hostility or manipulation," Rocky said, the image of the child Catherine had been always so clear in his mind.

"It's a problem for you though, isn't it?" asked Beatrice, "telling me how you feel."

"Yes," Rocky admitted. He was reluctant to make his admission; it seemed somehow unmanly. When he was younger, his feelings would have spurted out angrily. With age he found anger as upsetting as the real or imagined slights that produced his injured feelings.

Withdrawal had seemed a more judicious course of action than speaking out.

I'm not a mind reader, you know," said Beatrice gently. "At least when you'd go on a tirade, I knew what had bothered you."

Rocky forced a smile. "And most of the time it wasn't something you'd said or done, but you took the brunt of it."

"Oh, I'm not looking to go back to that mode," Beatrice said quietly but emphatically, "but it would help if you wouldn't suppress your feelings all the time. You may think that your responses to every situation are obvious, but they're not. Our friend Dave Christiansen used to say not to underestimate the obvious. Good advice but of no help if things aren't obvious."

"It's not hard to see where your daughter and granddaughter get their sensitivity to emotional climates," Rocky said. He was feeling uncomfortable, perhaps because the dialogue had more truth to it than he was comfortable with.

"Oh, there are enough baby feelings to go around in this family," Beatrice said. She came around the table to where Rocky was sitting and kissed him on top of the head. Standing behind him, she curled her arms around his neck and said, "I love you."

"Still? Amazing," offered Rocky playfully. "I love you too," Rocky said. He couldn't remember the last time he'd offered that response. It had been even longer, he was sure, since he had initiated the simple exchange before she had. Patting the hands she had folded over his chest, Rocky said, "But I ought to be doing something to earn it. I had better start getting that money together so we can start the Dave and Carla Christiansen Memorial Scholarship Endowment. That was a great idea you had, Treece, but not surprising coming from you, a woman who produces generations of women with baby feelings."

Beatrice leaned down and kissed his forehead, "I don't suppose you've considered that those girls might get some of their feelings from their father?"

Rocky gave his wife a wide-eyed look. "Please don't slander my off-spring."

"Your impossible," said Beatrice.

"Precisely my point," said Rocky. He made that recognition with renewed awareness that he must adjust to that reality, since he wouldn't be going anywhere other than where he was now.